BURIED
SECRETS

BY **CARLY ANNE WEST**
ART BY **TIM HEITZ AND**
ARTFUL DOODLERS LTD.

Scholastic Inc.

PROLOGUE

My grandma, Bubbe Fein, used to call them dust devils. It seemed like a weirdly sinister way to refer to the small cyclones that skipped across the vacant lot near the house she lived in with us. They didn't hurt anything except for maybe some ragweed or the occasional spider. But everything my grandmother named sounded a little menacing, so I never questioned it.

I was five years old the day she hid from me in that field. Up to that point, the vacant lot had been mine, a place to build a world I was in charge of. I'd drift past the edges of the property, even though my parents told me not to, but it wasn't on purpose. It was never on purpose.

That day, though, Bubbe followed me out there when I wasn't looking. She found a tree at the back of the lot where the brush hadn't yet been cleared away for the next house, and she formed her body to the back of the trunk because my grandma was just that small and her spine was just that crooked. She must have been there for more than an hour, watching me while I invented superheroes and destroyed imaginary cities with my inhuman powers. Occasionally, I'd swear I smelled rose perfume, the scent I'd come to associate with her, but as quickly as it would appear, it would dissipate into the fading daylight.

She waited until dusk—that hazy gray time after the sun gives up and the moon takes over—to strike. I'd wandered to the edge again, out of the range of supervision. I could hardly see the roofline of my house.

At first, I thought the tree beside me had come to life. My quick imagination couldn't quite make sense of the movement. Her long, age-spotted fingers closed around my wrist so fast, I couldn't even form a scream. She yanked me deeper into the brush, her square teeth clacking over her words as she curled her lips back.

"How far would you go?" she hissed.

I opened my mouth to answer, but instead, the delayed cry came out, and Bubbe cupped her other hand over my mouth, choking me with the stench of roses.

"You would scare your parents even more by screaming! Where are they, do you suppose? How frantic do you think they must be, searching high and low for you? Did the grocery store teach you nothing?"

They were all questions, but I didn't know how I was supposed to answer them. All I knew was that the hand she was squeezing tingled and the back of my throat was starting to burn.

I knew that nothing terrified me more than being alone with Bubbe Fein.

The dust devils that swirled in the vacant lot twirled their way toward the edge of the clearing, as though maybe to rescue me, but they broke apart the moment they hit the brush, leaving nothing but a thin coating of dust over my shoes.

My grandma curved her spine even lower to bring her face level to my own. Her hazel eyes had little triangles of marine blue and forest green, broken up like pieces of a pie. Her eyes always looked watery and red-rimmed, but I'd never see her cry. Not once.

Her bottom lip quivered as she spoke: "Maybe you wander because you'd prefer to be all alone."

She showed me her teeth again, and her eyes widened. It was the most awful smile I'd ever seen.

"That must be it. You want to be left all alone."

Releasing my wrist, Bubbe backed away, preparing to turn around toward the house. The dusk had given way to night in a blink, and suddenly, the edge of the brush, the vacant lot, and the comfort of home felt very far away.

"Bubbe, don't leave me alone," I pleaded.

"I'm sorry, Boychik, but this is what happens to little boys who wander," she said, her voice already fading as she kept walking away.

It should have been so easy to follow her out of the forest, but it felt impossible without a hand to hold, a grown-up to guide me through.

"Bubbe, I want to go home!"

But her voice was far, far away: "Those who wander are doomed to be left behind, Little Wolf. You'll get yourself lost, unless . . ."

And that was it. I'm sure she said something else. Of course she said something else. But forever after that dusk that turned to night, when she turned away from me and left me among the brush, I have never been able to recall the words she spoke.

All I remember is the back of her curved spine, and the way her footprints only left the faintest trail for me to follow home.

Chapter 1

wake with a gasp and startle everyone else in the car. My seat belt is damp with drool, and my head is sore from where I've been leaning against the window.

"Earth to Rumple-snore-skin," Enzo says, nudging my arm.

Enzo is next to me in the car, and I'm waiting for him to give me a hard time about the drool, but concern is tugging at the corners of his grin.

I slap on a smile and make myself chuckle. "Gotta get in my beauty sleep. You should try it sometime."

Enzo shoves me into the window, groaning but looking a little relieved. We don't say much else for the rest of the ride.

It's my birthday today, and for the first time in my life, I'm celebrating it with real-live friends. An occupational hazard of moving around so much is never landing in one place long enough to have anyone to invite to a party. I've had practically a year to think about it, and here's my grand conclusion: Raven Brooks is as weird as I am. Maybe that means I'm finally home.

We pull into the massive parking lot, and all of us pile out of the car, cracking our backs and groaning about the nearly three-hour car ride. I don't remember whose idea Spree Land was, but since it's my birth we're celebrating, I sense that the blame lies squarely with me.

"Not bad. We all managed to stay together for the whole trip. Think we had ourselves a real old-fashioned convoy!" Dad says, the only one not completely zonked from the trip.

"Jay, for the eightieth time, we're not getting a CB radio," Mom says, hauling the cake and gifts out of the car and distributing them among the rest of us to carry.

"I'm just saying, the open road is lonely," Dad says, pouting a little.

"Well, your inner long-haul trucker will just have to get used to the sound of his doting wife from here on out," Mom says, smooshing his face and giving him a kiss on his cheek while we stumble toward the ticket booth, our legs still adjusting to standing. I make a mental note to refurbish a CB radio from my stash for Dad.

Everyone's parents have come—Mr. and Mrs. Bales, Mr. Esposito, Mom and Dad. Trinity hangs back by her parents and gives me a warm smile, and I don't know how, but she must know I need it. I've been trying, but this winter was a lot to get over. Between the run-ins with Mr. Peterson, the involvement with police, and the evidence (well, what *should* have been evidence), the grown-ups have all agreed that the best thing to do is for the kids to simply move on.

Move on. It's that simple. Like passing a car accident on the side of the road. It was awful for someone else, and now it's time to focus on the traffic ahead. I look over at Maritza, who's had to go through this twice now—once with Lucy, and once with Mya. Was that why she looked so resigned? Was that why she wasn't screaming that, no matter how many searches we did on the weekends or Missing posters we put up, we *know* who was involved, all while the adults are sitting here doing nothing?

Mom and Dad even started taking me to see a therapist, a fun fact they've opted to keep from everyone else. They say it's to safeguard my privacy, but there's this tiny part of me that wonders who exactly they're protecting. Mom's still waiting on that funding from EarthPro, and Dad's only just smoothed things over with Mr. Esposito at the paper. I'm sure the last thing they want is everyone knowing their kid is a paranoid delinquent.

Oh, sorry. I'm a *highly sensitive adolescent prone to anxiety and heightened obsessive tendencies*, according to "Dr. Fern." I can never remember his name, so I just think of him as the guy with the office that smells like banana peels who sits next to this giant plastic fern tree. So that's his name now. Dr. Fern.

And the Fern is not completely wrong. I'm *highly*

sensitive to the fact that, despite a binder full of evidence, the police are still happy to believe that Mr. Peterson is simply an odd dude and his kids just ran away from their aunt's house for no good reason. I've got this *heightened paranoia* because the maniac across the street, aside from singing creepy nursery rhymes while chopping meat *alone* in his creepy house, knows that I'm onto him, enough to gather said *binder full of evidence* and give it to the police. And I'm *prone to anxiety* over the evidence I might've missed, all while watching the Missing posters of Aaron and Mya fade to nothing because it's just easier to "move on."

Yep. I must be crazy. Meanwhile, Mr. Peterson still lives across the street, hammering away for months now, power-drilling into Aliens-know-what, playing completely normal carnival music in the middle of the night.

"Okay, so cake first, right?" Mom says, breathless by the time we get to the Party Pavilion of Spree Land, which is more or less a covered patio area with overhead fans and picnic tables.

"I think we're gonna have to," says Mr. Bales. "It's likely to melt otherwise."

We rush through the singing and the candles, and I find that smile I used in the car, and I try—I *really* try—to be happy about the day. We're at an amusement park that hasn't been burned down and abandoned. To my knowledge, no one has died here. And, sure, Mr. Peterson had a hand in building this park just like he had a hand in building about a billion other parks outside of Raven Brooks, but that doesn't mean his imprint on this place has to taint the day.

Mom slices the cake and gives Dad two plates.

"You're just going to try to sneak an extra slice anyway," Mom says. "Might as well skip the dramatics."

"Which is why you are a goddess," he says, putting his chin on her shoulder before taking a corner chair.

Just as we're lifting our respective forks, Mr. Esposito clears his throat and nods to my parents.

"I think we're forgetting something," he says, and my parents scurry to find two more chairs to place at the end of the table, ruffling the plastic tablecloth as they hurry around.

"Right," Dad says, getting the explanation over with as quickly as possible. "Miguel had a, um, an idea that might pay homage to some people who might be . . ."

He looks to my mom to find the right words, but she looks as helpless as Dad does.

"To remember that, erm . . ."

"To remind us that two friends are here in spirit," Mr. Esposito says, and now I get it.

Maritza looks at me, and if my face is the same color red as hers, then we're both trying to decide if we're embarrassed or furious.

There in spirit. As in *not* in real life. Because it's time to move on. For real this time.

Trinity and Enzo look at each other and then look at Maritza and me, and then at their laps because to look at the parents now would be to betray our anger over them deciding how we should be feeling.

We let the parents chat while the four of us eat in silence, then sprint out the door to the shouts of "Meet back here in two hours!"

As soon as we're out of earshot, Enzo chimes in.

"He was trying to help," he says about his dad.

"That wasn't helping," Maritza says, looking at the ground. She doesn't sound angry so much as tired.

"It's like they want to pretend nothing's happened," I say, getting more frustrated by the second.

Trinity puts her arm around Maritza's shoulders and holds her other hand up to me.

"I know," she says. "They're never going to feel the way

we feel, because they can never experience what we've experienced. But . . . you guys, they kinda have a point."

I'm preparing to battle with Trinity, but then Maritza says something surprising.

"I hate this feeling," she says, and maybe it's the sun's reflection, but I think her eyes might be watery. "I hate feeling angry all the time. Or worried. Or—helpless. I just want to miss her. That's all I want to feel."

Then I can't think of a thing to say, because what she's saying feels true. Maybe it is that simple. Maybe we just need to miss them without all the other stuff.

Maybe I really have been looking for trouble.

It turns out rides are a great way to spend the day, because after melting cake and fumbling parents, *not* talking was actually the best remedy. Screaming felt so much better.

By the end of the fourth hour, we decide we have time for one more ride.

"So, choose wisely," Trinity says, eyeing us all carefully to fully reflect the seriousness of this decision.

"Cobra Kingdom or Scream School," Enzo says, pointing to the map. "Those are my votes."

"Scream School all the way," says Trinity.

"The line for Cobra Kingdom is shorter," I say, my palms starting to sweat.

"Scream School," Maritza votes, and the girls lock arms because of course they side with each other. Enzo's my last hope. He can deadlock us. It would be swell to leave Spree Land without having a panic attack. Either I'm the only one who knows that Mr. Peterson designed that specific school-themed ride, or they're all doing a great job of conveniently forgetting that.

"Come on," Trinity pleads with Enzo. "Cobra Kingdom is lame. Mechanical snakes popping out of baskets. Oooooh, scary," she says, waving her hands in mock fear.

Enzo looks at me, and I know I've lost.

"Sorry, Nicky. Looks like we're going to school."

The line moves slowly, and I try my best to listen to Enzo drone on about the camping trip they're going to take with their dad, and how Trinity's parents are considering Guatemala for their next sabbatical, and I do everything I can to block out the shrieks coming from the dark tunnel at the mouth of Scream School.

It's just a ride. It's just a stupid ride.

But even from outside the tunnel, Mr. Peterson's handprints are all over the design: the swirling letters that look so much like the ones that spelled out "Rotten Core," the entrance that looks like an open mouth framed by a handlebar mustache, the unmistakable argyle background

12

that's meant to resemble a school uniform, but instead looks suspiciously like his sweater.

"... so we'll probably go to Table Rock instead, even though Lake of the Ozarks is way better."

"It's not way better. You just like it because you caught a fish. Like, one time. A single fish. Five years ago," Maritza says, eyes rolling.

"It was the size of my head!" Enzo says defensively.

Trinity sneaks a glance at me, slowly shaking her head. Siblings.

And I want to smile and shake my head, too. I want to tell Enzo I'm sure the fish was mutant huge. But the screams from inside the tunnel are growing louder, and we keep inching closer to the front, and why can't I let it go?

Why does the shadow of Mr. Peterson still loom so large?

"Four, please," Trinity says when we get to the front of the line. "Can we have desks next to each other?"

The ride operator shrugs and vaguely indicates to a row of old-fashioned wooden chairs with desks attached to their arms. The others grab the back three, leaving the one in the front row for me. I go to sit down, but the operator waves me to the one ahead of it, separated from the other three.

"That one's broken," he says.

I try to sit next to one of the others, but those rows have filled. The one lone seat in the front is all that's left.

"Looks like you're at the head of the class," Enzo says, snickering.

"Seriously?" I glower at him. We both know if anyone's the teacher's pet, it's him.

The entire ride is built to mimic a shuttered, abandoned schoolhouse. As though kids needed one more reason to dread school.

An alarm meant to simulate a school bell rips through the air and down my spine, and a menacing voice comes over the loudspeaker: "Take your seats, boys and girls. It's going to be a bumpy ride!"

I turn in my seat and find Maritza, and her face answers the question I can't form words to ask. Yes, that was indeed Mr. Peterson's voice. No doubt it was recorded during the making of the ride, long before Golden Apple Amusement Park was a glimmer in the mind of its inventor.

Still, that voice. *That voice.*

The ride lurches forward, and I tell myself over and over that I'm in Spree Land. This isn't another nightmare.

Darkness closes around us as we round the corner from the tunnel entrance, and I hear Enzo go, *"Oh man,"* and maybe he regrets not choosing Cobra Kingdom now, but he should have regretted it about two minutes ago.

"It's not even that scary," I hear Trinity say from somewhere behind me, but was that her voice catching, and why are we still sitting in pitch dark anyway? Shouldn't something be popping out at us or creeping up from behind?

"Is this part of the ride?" Maritza whispers, and at least I'm not imagining it. The ride jerks forward again, and I know I'm not the only one who jumped because that was definitely Enzo screaming before he could catch himself.

The desk seems to tighten across my waist, but that can't be right. I try to see if any of the others are struggling, but I can't even see my hand in front of me.

The track under me tips to a steep incline, and for a second, the pressure on my stomach eases as my back presses against the wooden chair. I take a deep breath in and try to think happy thoughts. Non-murderous-neighbor thoughts.

I'll get to open presents later. Presents are good.

There are still seven weeks of summer left. Summer is great.

My parents are finally starting to lay off the extra-curricular push now that I have a plan for a new club. Non-nagging parents are fantastic.

The track under me crests, the desk levels, and I try so hard not to think about that one rusted car stalled at the apex of the Rotten Core roller coaster right before Lucy Yi got thrown from the ride, but suddenly, there's a voice again over the loudspeaker, and a dim light radiates from the depths below the track.

"All right now, boys and girls, are you ready for your test?" Mr. Peterson's recorded voice echoes over the loudspeaker.

"Oh, I have major regrets," I hear Enzo whisper behind me, but just as he finishes "regrets," the bottom drops out from under us, and in a stomach-inverting second, we're soaring toward a dim blue light below, leveling out to a sudden stop that shoves the desk deeper into my gut, knocking the wind out of me long enough to black out for a second.

When I come to, I'm face-to-face with a ghostly white head, its features absent, its body long and unwieldy.

I've seen this mannequin before.

"No no no no no!" I hear myself say, but all I can feel is the pressure of the desk against my stomach, and no matter how hard I try, I can't wiggle out of the chair it's pinning me against.

The mannequin leans forward, and I'm powerless to move. Mr. Peterson's voice booms from above.

"Now, now, no cheating!"

Then the track pushes me forward, and I'm inches from the mannequin before the desk swivels to the left, snaking me through a dark hallway lined with rusted orange lockers, an overhead light flickering to reveal an impossibly tall figure at the end of the corridor.

It reaches its arms to the sides, revealing a silhouette of spindly fingers that scrape along the metal locks beside it.

The track moves my desk slowly toward the figure, but that only gives me more time to realize that I can't leave. I can't move. All I can do is sit here while this stupid ride brings me closer to whatever monster stands at the end of that hallway. I close my eyes and try to bring back the good thoughts, but what I see instead is a corridor lined with locked doors like the ones Aaron and I used to pick open at the Golden Apple Factory, back when things were less complicated and I was just that new kid from Charleston and everyplace else, not this kid who dreams about his dead grandma and sleepwalks through creepy forests and has a nervous breakdown on carnival rides because holy Aliens his unhinged neighbor made his kids disappear, and what's to stop him from making us disappear right here today on this ridiculously terrifying ride he built?

"It looks like someone just earned themselves a trip to the principal's office!" Mr. Peterson's voice menaces over the loudspeaker.

"Enzo?" I call. "Trinity?" But hearing the panic in my voice only makes me panic more.

Nobody answers, and the desk is so tight against my waist, I can't even turn around. It doesn't matter, though. I'm the first in line. I'm the first to see the "principal."

In a display of total betrayal, my eyes refuse to shut as I draw closer to the end of the corridor, and just as the face of the monster begins to emerge from the shadows, my desk jerks right, and I'm in what is presumably the cafeteria, but what's actually a steaming swamp with some lunch tables rotting away in murky water. Steam shoots from all corners of the big room, revealing just how many hidden corners there are, and each time the steam fires, it's like something is breathing on my ankles, leaving behind an unsettling dampness.

Suddenly, there's skittering all around me, and as the sound reaches fever pitch, it collects into the galloping sound of one heaving giant lurching toward me.

The desk speeds along its track and leaves the cafeteria and its lurking giant behind before bursting into the library, another mannequin greeting me too closely, its faceless head sporting glasses on a string of pearls, its hand up to its nonexistent mouth.

"Shhhhhh," it admonishes, and I oblige because let's be honest, I couldn't form words if I wanted to. Bookshelves rattle and tip forward and backward under the rumble of something even farther underground than we are, and moldy books spill from the shelves to the ground, slapping the floor loudly and stirring up a sea of more faceless mannequins, each with a book in their hand as they slowly emerge from behind the shelves that are still standing. They move toward me with blind persistence, and my desk—my stupid, stupid desk on its stupid, stupid track—forces me forward until I'm nose–to–non-nose with one of them, my mouth gulping air instead of screaming like it should.

Finally, the nightmare librarian backs away, and the desk speeds along its track toward a grate that looks terrifyingly similar to one of those dungeon grates with spikes that fit neatly into holes in the ground. The ride speeds up, and I'm headed straight for the gate, and there's no way I could stop in enough time to keep from smashing headfirst into the bars. This time I do scream, and finally, I hear screaming behind me, but none of that matters because we're all going to be a pile of grated kids in a moment, and why? Why couldn't we have just gone with the snake ride?

I try to turn around to see Enzo. Maybe I just want a familiar face. Maybe I don't want the very last thing I see in my short life to be the rusted gate of Scream School. But the desk is too tight against me, and all I can manage is a half turn.

And that's when I see him.

There, in a corner almost entirely hidden by faux brick and metal gears no one riding the ride is really supposed to see—is a pair of wide green eyes practically glowing over a waxy, curled mustache.

"No," I whisper, because how could that actually be? How could Mr. Peterson be here, right here where I'm about to breathe my last breath, on my birthday of all days? How is he here, watching *with actual glee* as I hurtle toward my death?

Just when I think he's going to answer the question in my eyes, he slowly backs away, and the shadows swallow him into the background of the ride he created.

My desk screeches to a stop, shifting backward before moving again, this time on an incline headed toward daylight.

My desk crawls to its final stop, where it started, the bored attendant loosening a pin beside me that I don't remember him tightening before the ride. The pressure on my stomach eases, and I shove the desk away on its hinge and stumble from the chair.

"You guys. You guys!" I clamor to tell the others about my Mr. Peterson sighting, but they're giving Enzo a hard time about screaming.

"It was a yell, not a scream. There's a difference," he says.

"You could've broken glass," Trinity says, and she and Maritza dissolve into a giggle fit.

"It was Nicky, too!" Enzo says, pulling me under the bus with him. But I don't care about that right now.

"Dude, are you gonna puke? You look like you're gonna puke," Enzo says to me, and the girls stop laughing and nod.

"Yeah, he's in the pre-vomit stage," Trinity says. "And we're in the splash zone."

Maritza takes a step back, and the others join her.

"I'm not going to barf," I say, but I can't get the rest out because the attendant is ambling toward us, looking irritated that he had to walk several steps toward us.

"Hey!" he calls, as though just a few more feet would tax him. He holds his hand out to Trinity. "You left this."

He extends his hand, which holds a folded piece of paper. From the top of the fold, it looks like a really well-done drawing, not the kind someone would just abandon. At first glance, I think it might be one of those caricatures people pay to have drawn. I remember seeing a booth near the entrance.

"That's not mine," Trinity says politely, but the attendant is having none of it.

He sighs. "First row in front of the broken chair?"

"Oh, that was Nicky," she says, nodding to me.

"Not mine," I say.

"Well, it's not mine, either," he says, and it's clear he has no intention of keeping the paper that's been abandoned on the seat of his ride.

"Um, I guess we could take it to Lost and Found?" Trinity offers, and the attendant shrugs and leaves without another word.

"Oookay," Trinity says. "Anyone have any idea where the Lost and Found might be?"

We all shake our heads, but Maritza continues to stare at

the paper. "What's it say?" she asks tentatively. "I'm not sure we should open it if it's not ours," Trinity says.

But it's like Maritza is in a trance. She carefully takes the paper from Trinity and unfolds it like some unearthed artifact from an ancient civilization. She must have already seen what the rest of us are seeing now.

"Is that . . . ?" Enzo starts.

"Their Missing poster," Trinity finishes, her voice quiet.

As I walk around Maritza and peer at the flip side of the poster, I get a better look at what I thought was the caricature. Instead, what I see is a heavily shaded charcoal sketch of a tree. The pine is impossibly tall and towers over the tiniest figure of what looks like a boy. He's crouched at the base of the trunk, his head buried in his knees, his hands behind his neck.

It's not *what* the picture depicts that makes my stomach flip, though. It's the style of the drawing. There's no mistaking that the hand behind this drawing is the same one that sketched those dozens of pictures in the makeshift art studio under the canvas shelter behind the factory.

"Why would anyone use one of these to doodle on?" Enzo asks. "That's messed up."

"You know, I thought it was just my imagination, but I'd swear these went missing from the library. I thought maybe it just fell down, but . . ." Trinity says, her brow crinkling as she stares at the poster.

Maritza stops staring at the paper and turns to me. "Nicky, why did you have this?"

I try not to hear her tone as accusatory, but it's pretty much impossible.

"Wait, what?"

"It was in your seat," she says.

"You don't actually believe that ride operator, do you?" I ask, my voice pitching a little higher than I mean for it to. But why is she looking at me like that?

Enzo takes a step toward Maritza and puts his hand over the Missing poster, as though to protect us all from the harm it might cause.

"That guy was about as sharp as a spoon," Enzo says, looking back at Scream School. "He probably got you mixed up with the toddler who was wailing at the exit," he says, jabbing me in the rib as he takes the paper from Maritza's hands.

"*You* were screaming," Trinity says as she pushes Enzo toward the Lost and Found. "We all heard you screaming."

We make our way toward the front of the park, but Maritza hangs back.

"Hey, you okay?" I ask her, and just like that, her trance breaks.

While she was under her spell, though, something changed. Suddenly, she's looking at me like she's never seen me before in her life.

"Uh, you in there?" I ask, waving my hand in front of her face, and she flinches from me, taking a quick step back.

"Whoa," I say. "I know, the ride made me jumpy, too, okay?"

I look for Enzo and Trinity, but they're already up ahead in pursuit of the Lost and Found.

"I need to tell you something," I say, because if anyone will understand, it's Maritza. "I know this is gonna sound crazy, but I think I saw something in there."

I look for all the usual reactions from her—the spark in her wide eyes, the way she tips her head to the side just a tiny bit, the quick look around to make sure there's no one else listening. All the things she did that day in the woods last fall, when she finally confessed that she had the same suspicions that Aaron and Mya Peterson weren't really living in Minnesota with their aunt.

She doesn't do any of those things, though. Instead, she looks for Trinity and Enzo. Then she takes another step away from me. Then another.

"Yeah, I'm . . . um . . . I'm going to the ticket counter," she says, then turns on her heel and runs to catch up to the others, leaving me alone to wonder what I did to make Maritza look at me like that.

Like I was suddenly a suspect instead of a friend.

Chapter 2

Trinity nudges the last yellowtail roll toward me.

We're at our new favorite hangout, Nigiri Nights, a place that pretty much covers all the bases: It feeds our insatiable sushi appetite, we can always find an open table (except on bingo night), and the foods are blissfully cold. Thanks to a summer of record-breaking heat and our parents' not-so-subtle encouragement to explore "other interests" (i.e., NOT Mr. Peterson), Nigiri Nights has become the unofficial headquarters for the planning of our newest undertaking: an engineering club.

"All I want is a freezing-cold pool and a twenty pack of ice pops," Enzo complains.

"The blue ones are mine," Maritza teases, but the usual bite in her tone is missing. It might have melted sometime this afternoon like Dad's entire box of Ho Hos, may they rest in peace.

"Not a chance. The blue ones are the best ones and you know it," Enzo shoots back.

"Could we stop arguing over hypothetical ice pops and

get down to the subject at hand?" Trinity says, abandoning her trademark diplomacy. "And, Nicky, you have T-minus five seconds to eat that last yellowtail before it's mine."

I hold my hands up in surrender, and she snatches it with her lacquered chopsticks. I'm normally the Yellowtail King, but I don't have much of an appetite.

Aside from the heat, I'm nervous. Maritza hasn't said a single word to me since we got here. In fact, I'm struggling to remember a full sentence she's aimed in my direction that hasn't burned just a little since my birthday at Spree Land. Usually, as the two lefties of the group, we'd gravitate to the same side of the table to avoid bumping elbows with the person next to us. Now she's crowded in next to Enzo and Trinity, leaving me on my own while I sit across from them.

I can tell Enzo and Trinity notice the change, too, but if they think it's weird, they sure don't want to risk saying anything about it.

And I don't see either of them grabbing the seat next to me.

"We need a name," Enzo says after he drains his soda and muffles a burp. "Something catchy."

"Well, then we're going to have to leave the word 'engineering' out of it," I say.

"What's wrong with 'engineering'?" Enzo asks, genuinely wounded.

"Hey, *I* know what's cool about it. I'm just saying I'm not sure how many kids are going to be scrambling for a spot on a club that meets after school to take apart old radios and do math problems."

I know I should be more supportive of Enzo's idea. I mean, it's obvious he tried to think up something we'd all like doing, something that puts our former sleuthing to more . . . er . . . wholesome use. If it were up to him, we'd probably be trying to start a gaming club or something, but Trinity really wants something for her college application . . . even if college is quite a ways away. And as for me, picking locks and rigging binocuscopes feels like a huge waste of time now that we've all agreed to give up hope that Aaron and Mya are ever coming back.

"No one's making you do anything," Maritza says, finally looking me in the eye.

She holds my gaze for maybe a half a second before looking back down at her wasabi and ginger, her cheeks glowing pink.

"Okay, let's take a step back, everyone," Trinity says, regaining some of her mediation mojo, but she looks like she hasn't slept in days, and suddenly, it occurs to me that no one seems to be excited about Nigiri Nights anymore.

"Sorry, Enzo. I didn't mean to tank your idea," I say, not sure if I mean it, but right now, the only one who seems happy with me being at the table is Enzo, and maybe an engineering club wouldn't be so bad. At one point, I think I was even kind of excited about it.

"So, we keep 'engineering' in the name, just so people know what it is," I say, and Enzo perks up a little.

"But the rest has to be memorable," he says.

"How about Totally Reliable Incomes of the U.S.?" Trinity quips. "TRIUS!"

"Cute," I say, "but it's missing 'engineering.'"

"Engineering: We Make Geeking Out Look Good," Maritza says, joining in the fun of ridiculing Enzo and me.

"That's more of a slogan," Enzo says, then shoves his sister. "And we *do* make it look good."

"I feel like we need a superhero theme," I say, and no one makes fun of me, so we run with it.

"Engineer Men!" Enzo says, puffing out his chest.

"Uh," Trinity arches an eyebrow at him.

"Well, it kind of loses its magic to say Engineering Men *or Women*," he says, his chest deflating.

"Engineers League?" Maritza tries.

"That sounds like a labor union," says Enzo, and we all grow quiet.

"Engineering Masters of the Universe," I say.

We all mumble it to ourselves.

"It's good, but it doesn't exactly roll off the tongue," Trinity says.

"No prob. EMU for short," I say.

They look at me, uncertain.

"Like those ostrich-looking things?" says Maritza.

"Sure, why not?" I say. "Those birds can be vicious."

Enzo is the first one to crack. He laughs so hard he practically chokes on the tiny drops of soda he's managed to slurp from his cup. "Yeah, they can tear you limb from limb with their tiny wings," he says.

Trinity breaks next: "You know, I heard they were bred for hunting lions," she

Possible Club Names

~~Totally Reliable Incomes of the U.S. — TRITUS!~~

~~Engineering: We Make Geeking Out Look Good~~

~~Engineer Man~~

~~Engineer Man or Woman~~

~~Engineers League~~

Engineering Masters of the Universe (EMU)

says, and Maritza and I can't help ourselves because it's been a while since we all laughed, and holy Aliens does it feel good.

"We should start an emu farm!" Maritza says.

"This town is so weird, I'm surprised it doesn't already have one," Enzo says.

"We already have a llama farm, so why not?" Trinity exclaims, and one by one, we all stop laughing.

Because everyone knows about Aaron and me stealing the St. Nick's Lovely Llamas sign, and now we're right back to where we always end up no matter how hard we try to avoid it—remembering that Aaron and Mya are missing.

"I mean, it's still a good name," Enzo says, and maybe because we're all just eager for this night to be over, we silently agree that:

1. The club will be the Engineering Masters of the Universe.
2. The mystery of where Aaron and Mya went will never be solved.
3. And for some reason, I'm on thin ice with Maritza.

That's okay, though. I enjoyed almost a year of not being a professional-level loser, and maybe that's all some of us get in life.

Just as we're all getting up to leave, Enzo reminds Maritza that they have to meet their dad at the coffee shop later, and Maritza couldn't look more relieved to not have to walk home with me.

Outside, rippling under a dusky breeze, a yellowing and faded Missing poster clings to the streetlight, the same tired-eyed picture of Aaron, listing his last known whereabouts as though anyone was really paying attention; the same snapshot of Mya, her chin resting on the palm of her hand, elbows bent atop a desk. The classic school portrait.

I'm halfway down the street before I feel a tug on the

back of my shirt, and I turn to find Trinity, hands on her hips, waiting for me to say something.

When I don't, she rolls her eyes.

"Do I have to feel sorry for you to join this pity party?"

I feel my cheeks get hot. "I don't—who said anything about—?"

"'Cause I didn't bring a present or anything," she says, the corner of her mouth curling almost imperceptibly.

I turn back around and keep walking, doing my best not to show how happy I am that at least one of my friends is willing to walk home with me.

"I'm not imagining it," I say, and Trinity's quiet. "It's like . . . it's like she's afraid of me or something," I go on, struggling with the silence Trinity seems so comfortable in. She walks with long, even strides, and all I can hear besides our footsteps is the gentle clacking of the beads at the ends of her braids.

I'm suddenly aware of how dark it is. We'd been in the sushi place longer than I realized, and even though the night is blissfully cooler than the afternoon was, no one is out enjoying it. Friendly Court is a barren landscape.

"She's not afraid . . . not exactly," Trinity says, and I didn't even realize we'd stopped walking. Her voice startles me out of my trance, and I find her eyes searching mine.

"What do you mean 'not exactly'?"

"It's just . . ." she struggles, and I think this is the first time I've seen Trinity at a loss for the right words.

"Just say it," I say, trying to put us both out of our misery. I was happy for her company, but now all I want to do is crawl into bed and lay on top of the covers until the rest of the day's heat leaves me.

"I mean, is it possible that maybe she feels like you haven't really let it go?" Trinity creeps up on the answer like she might startle it away.

I push my palm into my forehead until it hurts and squeeze my eyes against the bright white light the pressure creates. When I open my eyes, Trinity looks worried.

I throw my hands in the air because I can't believe I'm having this conversation again, with the same friend who knows everything I know, who has seen all the evidence I've seen.

"Seriously?"

"C'mon, Nicky. You know I'm right."

"Of course you're right!"

Trinity's forehead creases. She's worried. About me. About the only one who isn't acting like nothing happened.

"I've slipped into the Twilight Zone," I mutter, walking away.

Trinity follows stubbornly. "Nicky—"

"Or maybe the Aliens," I rant. "They finally did it. They finally abducted me. And now I'm in a simulated world where everyone ignores what's RIGHT IN FRONT OF THEM!"

"Nicky, get a grip!" Trinity scolds, and I'm powerless to defy her because this is the first time I've seen Trinity angry, *actually* angry, and I wonder if Enzo's ever seen her mad because this will likely be the first and only time I cross Trinity.

"No one is saying they don't see it, okay? No one is telling you you're crazy. Although I have my theories," she says, her voice lower now, but her eyes still burning a hole through me.

"All we're saying—all Maritza can't say because she's too nice—is that you shouldn't be the one to solve it."

I absorb her words like punches, flexing against each one, but I only have the strength to hunch down and block.

"You're not a detective, Nicky. None of us are."

But it shouldn't take a detective to say when something is this wrong, and I know Trinity knows it because we're several houses down from my house, and even though I'm looking at her, she's looking across the street in the direction of the Peterson house.

Because she hasn't exactly let it go, either.

Soon, though, I realize she isn't just staring at the Peterson house like I thought she was. She's staring at what's *coming* from the Peterson house.

A beam of light hits the middle of the street in starts and stops, a pool of bright white on the inky asphalt. It appears, then disappears, then appears again, its rhythm unsteady. It looks like an accident.

But somehow, I know it's not random.

"Are we both seeing this?" Trinity whispers.

"You mean that bright blinking light aimed right at my house coming from across the street?" I whisper back, transfixed. "Yeah, I'm seeing that."

"It might not be anything," Trinity says, but she knows as well as I do that it definitely means something.

We stare at the light like moths, frightened to move forward but taking slow steps anyway, inching midway down the block where my house stares at the Peterson house. More specifically, where *I* stare at the Peterson house. This is the sign I've been waiting for, the proof that's eluded me for almost a year.

Until now. Because now that we're just two houses away from mine, there's no doubt where the light is coming from.

"That's Aaron's room," I say, and Trinity reaches for my wrist and squeezes it hard enough to hurt.

"You're sure?"

"Positive."

She squeezes my wrist harder, and I feel my fingertips starting to tingle as they lose blood.

"Is that a—?"

"It looks like a flashlight."

"But it's flashing on and off. It's almost like—"

"It's a pattern," I say, my voice barely above a whisper.

"Is it?"

"It's definitely a pattern."

It only takes another second to decipher what the pattern is.

"SOS," I say.

"How do you even know that?" Trinity breathes.

"Everybody knows that," I whisper back, and even though we're barely making any noise, she shushes me.

I take another few steps forward, and Trinity starts to follow before I hold my hand up, keeping my eyes on the window.

I turn to her, and now she's looking up at the pool of light reflecting on the blacktop between Aaron's house and mine. Trinity's eyes grow bigger, and I whip back around to see why. There in the spotlight, a hulking figure takes shape, its shoulders touching each end of the light's circle.

The light dances spastically in the road for less than a second before, all at once, it goes dark, the light snuffed out as suddenly as it appeared.

I run the rest of the distance on the sidewalk before Trinity can stop me.

"Aaron," I call out, and Trinity catches me, slapping her hand over my mouth before I can make another sound.

"It was him!" I protest through her fingers, trying in vain to wriggle out of her grip. Trinity pulls me behind the hedge separating my house from the one next door, wrestling me to the ground and pinning my shoulders so I can't get up.

"You saw it! It was him!" I sputter, dead grass scratching my spine.

"Even if it was, that shadow sure wasn't his," Trinity whispers frantically, and I know that, but how can she be okay with just doing nothing?

"Stop being stupid!" she hisses, and since when was she this mean? But that's not anger on her face. That's pure terror. Then I remember that I'm not the only one who's come face-to-face with those wild eyes and that tightly curled mustache. Trinity has, too. We all have.

Tom, Tom, the piper's son,
Stole a pig and away did run.

I stop fighting because I know she's right. Whatever was making that light flash, we know for sure what made it stop. It's the same person who chased us into the night with a shovel six months ago.

Trinity and I sit on the lawn behind the hedge and stare up at the darkened window that used to be Aaron's—that might still be Aaron's. We stare for so long that my eyes start to burn, and Trinity starts to shiver under the nighttime breeze that's kicked up. When tiny droplets start to dot the sidewalk in front of us, we finally stand up, brushing the grass from our backsides and meeting each other's eyes for the first time since that flashlight beam poured onto the street.

"I'll walk you home if you want," I say, and normally Trinity would roll her eyes and tell me she's tougher than me, and she's right. But this time she lets me, and I try not to show her how scared I am to walk back home by myself.

Once I leave Trinity's, I take a shortcut behind the alley—the one I took with Aaron after we stole Farmer Llama's sign—and slow my pace the second I round the corner onto Friendly Court, now the unfriendliest court I think I've ever walked.

Once again behind the hedge across the street, I creep around the bristling shrub and edge toward my house, reaching silently for the house key in my pocket, pretending not to care about making any noise. When my trembling hands drop my key, though, my heart thrums like a hummingbird as I crouch to the sidewalk and pick it up, kicking aside a stray rubber ball that's rolled onto the walkway.

It takes me three tries to unlock the front door, probably because I'm looking over my shoulder the entire time instead of at the lock. When the bolt finally slides, I lean into the door and take a giant inhale against the other side, locking the handle and the dead bolt, then checking it twice before running up the stairs.

The flicker from the TV in my parents' room lights the way to my room, and I'm mildly comforted by their soft snoring sounds and the chatter of whatever program they couldn't stay awake through. The light from the streetlamp shines bright in my room, and I immediately spy the chocolate frosted mini Bundt cake plated on my desk, a note tucked under the edge.

FINDING THE STRENGTH TO MOVE ON IS HARD. YOU DESERVE A SOFT CAKE. WE'RE PROUD OF YOU, NARF.

I have no idea where they went for dinner tonight, but it was supposed to be just for them. And they thought of me. They thought about how proud they are of me.

For moving on.

I stare at the perfectly molded dessert. It doesn't even have to try; it can't help but look delicious. I pick up the fork my parents left for me and slice into the cake, and oh sweet Aliens it's even softer than I thought it would be. Maybe it could really be that easy—that sweet—to simply forget.

The fork is inches from my mouth before it stops, midair. I can smell the chocolate right under my nose. It smells perfect. But for the first time in my life, I don't want dessert.

I set the fork back on the plate, letting the bite fall against the rest of the cake.

Walking to my bedroom window, I cup my hands against the glass and peer at the window across the street that moments before screamed a silent plea.

Before the scream was muffled. Or worse.

I look at the cake on my desk, then back at the window, then at the cake.

"Why did it have to be chocolate?" I sigh.

I pull the shades on my window, then sit at my desk. I take a pen from the drawer, and when I can't find any paper, I put my hand on the note from Mom and Dad and slide it toward me. With a deep breath, I turn the paper over and write.

1) PICTURES BY FACTORY: WHO IS THE ARTIST? WHO TOOK THEM AWAY?

2) BACKYARD: WHAT DID MR. P BURY LAST SUMMER? THIS SUMMER?

3) BASEMENT??

4) IF AARON IS IN THE WINDOW . . .

I blink hard, trying not to write the last bit, but there's no other question to ask.

If Aaron was in the window . . . where is Mya?

I stare at my list of questions, the impression of my parents' words still visible from the other side of the paper.

"I'm sorry, Mom and Dad," I say to the words, my voice barely a whisper. Because if there's one thing video games and comic books have taught me, it's that with great power comes great responsibility. And if no one else is willing to help Aaron and Mya, I know I have to.

My list is bold-lettered and impossible. Every question's answer feels utterly out of reach.

Except for maybe one.

I tap my pen a few times on the question before circling it, as though maybe to make it a little more possible.

When I go to bed that night, I still see my hand circling the word "backyard," making an impression in my brain like my pen made on the paper.

Chapter 3

There's new dirt, and there's old dirt, Bubbe Fein used to say.

New dirt lets the fingers dig and pull. New dirt leaves spaces in between the granules. But old dirt . . . old dirt keeps its secrets held tight. You scratch and you scratch, but all you'll ever uncover is the fleshy tips of your fingers. You'll scratch and you'll scratch, but that old dirt will never let you in.

You scratch and you scratch, Boychik, and you'll find nothing but dust.

I should be thinking about a million other things as I kneel in the dirt in the shadow of Mr. Peterson's house.

I should be thinking about what a terrible, dangerous idea this is, or how unlikely it is I'll find anything that will help me save Aaron and Mya. And what if I do find something? Maybe I should be thinking about what sort of horrors I might dig up in the backyard I was so focused on plunging my shovel into.

Maybe I should be thinking about Mr. Peterson . . . about what he'll do if he finds me.

But no. Instead, I'm staring at the once-again bald patch of ground that seems to be my neighbor's favorite burial site. And I'm thinking about my dead grandmother's insane rantings.

The night is windy. The leaves on the giant tree in the front yard rustle with each passing breeze, but I'm more focused on the muffled drilling I can hear coming from the basement. I'm hoping the noise will mask some of the sound of my work.

I've come prepared: I have a tool for digging, tools for detecting, tools for excavating. I have every enhanced invention a budding engineer could ask for. In other words, I have everything I need to do the one thing I shouldn't be doing.

I lay my bag of high-powered binoculars and infrared heat detector and seismically altered magnet and microwave redirector down on the ground with the care that delicate machinery deserves. I have no idea what I'm going to find in this yard, but whatever it is, I'm going to be ready.

What I didn't bring is anything to defend myself with in case Mr. Peterson stops whatever he's doing and finds me.

I lean on my pogo-powered shovel and wince as it creaks under my weight. Had I been thinking, I might have oiled its springs ahead of time. Of course, had I been thinking, I might not have hopped Mr. Peterson's crumbling picket fence in the first place.

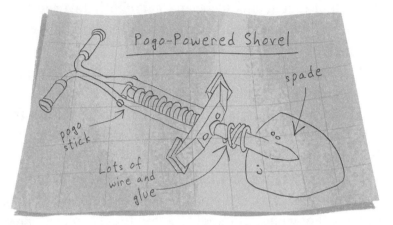

"Now or never, Narf," I whisper to myself, and wait for the next big wind before thrusting the shovel's blade into the dirt, the pogo handle supplying an extra-powerful dig.

With each new exhale of wind, I plow deeper into the backyard grave, my thirst for answers overtaking the fear any sane person should be feeling. I'm so caught up in the rhythm of the progress of the shovel, I barely notice that the drilling has stopped, and the excited squeak of the pogo handle chirps high into the night, echoing on the suddenly still air.

The moon is bright, and it only makes me feel more exposed, but after the next wind sweeps across the yard, I once again grip the handle of a pogo stick I bounced on exactly two times before it chipped my tooth and decided it could serve a better purpose.

I grip that pogo handle like it's Thor's hammer, preparing to bring it down to the ground with epic purpose. Just then, I feel a tickle on my wrist and turn it over to find a spider the size of my palm skittering down my hand.

I throw the shovel and let out an involuntary shout. Okay, it was a scream. Anyway, it was loud.

Holding my breath, I stare at the back of the Peterson house, waiting for some sign that I woke the evil inside.

This is a horrible, horrible idea, I tell myself. Of course it's a horrible idea. It would be stupid even if this *wasn't* Mr. Peterson's house.

I look from the basement door to the shovel to my house, then back to the door, the shovel, my house.

Is it possible that maybe she feels like you haven't really let it go?

Finding the strength to move on is hard.

You'll find nothing but dust, Boychik.

Then I remember something else—the flicker of a light emanating from the window of a boy I told myself was gone. A series of flickers like the blinking of a very alive eye.

"A little dirt never hurt anyone," I say to the shovel, and against every ounce of judgment, I continue digging.

It doesn't take me long. The shovel scrapes against something soft, and I wince at the possibility of what it could be. But when I move the shovel a little to the left, it knocks against something hard.

Still, the dirt holds its treasure tight, and no matter how many ways I try to clear it away, I can't seem to find any edge to the object.

I drag my bag of tricks over to the hole I've dug and begin rifling through. I don't have to search for long before the solution jumps out at me.

It nearly hits me in the head.

I discovered how to hyperpower a magnet by accident (a long story involving an iron bar and a whole spool of wire coiling), but the result is an insanely powerful magnet that, if I'm not careful, can act like a caged animal set free.

Which is what it does now.

The magnet is in the hole before I've had a chance to catch it, and it's discovered for me a metal rivet attached to a handle. When I move the magnet just a little, another handle erupts from the earth.

"Okay, magnet, do your magic."

With three hard yanks, I unearth what looks to be a canvas duffel bag.

Just then, because apparently my brain hates me, a memory flashes before me of Mr. Peterson wielding a meat cleaver above a lump of beef, and please, please, please don't let there be anything resembling a meat cleaver in here. *Please.*

But when I move the bag around, I'm surprised at the sound the contents make: like plastic clattering together.

"What the—?"

I unzip the bag to find coils of celluloid piled like curls cut from a doll's head. Some still have pieces of VHS attached to them. Others have lost their original casings altogether. My dad has taken enough home videos for me to see what these used to be. It's a buried bag full of busted memories.

Then, before I even hear anything, the hairs on the back of my neck stand at attention.

The slow creak of a door groans somewhere nearby. I stand motionless in the yard, the bag of VHS pieces tight in my grasp. I hold my breath and wait for another sound, but whoever made the door creak must be holding their breath, too.

Suddenly, I feel the weight of the bag shift, and a large piece of plastic comes tumbling out of the opening, clattering against the other pieces before landing with a soft thud on the ground.

It wasn't that loud. It wasn't loud enough for anyone to hear.

Right?

But I'm unconvinced enough to hastily push the freshly dug dirt back into the hole I've made. I find the clumps of grass that used to cover the surface, the blades still clinging to enough dirt for me to smoosh them back together in a kind of lawn jigsaw puzzle.

I'm just noting the sound of my wheezing breath, when I hear a different kind of noise—the kind a boot makes on a step. The kind of sound a large man like Mr. Peterson would make if he were, say, to come out in the middle of the night to find the neighbor kid covered in dirt next to a shovel, digging up his yard and holding whatever it is that he wanted desperately to destroy but couldn't quite get rid of.

I don't remember crouching to grab the fallen piece of cassette. I don't remember how my palms got scraped up or how I got grass in my hair. I don't even remember how I lost my supercharged magnet. All I remember is the feeling of the wind on my face. I remember slinging the bag's strap across my body, and I remember the scratch of the bushes from the yard next door to my house. It's like I don't even return to my body until I'm in my own backyard, stuffing the duffel bag of buried secrets under the back porch.

After sitting crouched behind my supply bag in the backyard for what feels like half the night, I work up the nerve to stand. Then I gather a little more courage and edge toward the fence that separates my front yard from the back. Peering carefully over the fence, I brace myself for the sight of Mr. Peterson, searching his own yard for the intruder he heard . . . or searching *my* yard for the intruder he already suspects.

When I peek over the fence, what I see instead is a street full of empty yards. All of Friendly Court is asleep except for me.

But that's not possible.

"I heard him. I know I heard him," I whisper, but all I hear are the ramblings of a paranoid kid who shouldn't be paranoid anymore.

In fact, it seems that nothing is working out the way I'm told it's supposed to. The feeling of missing Aaron should have gone away a long time ago, according to the therapist. The drive toward finding a productive hobby or at least promising extracurricular activity should be stronger, at least according to my parents. My suspicion of Mr. Peterson should be less important than my fear of him, at least according to my friends.

Clearly, I'm not anything I should be.

Except that I'm a boy who should be in bed, the covers tucked in at the sides, the ridges of my fingernails clean of old dirt that shouldn't have let me find anything, according to my dead bubbe.

But the dirt did let me find something, and though I have no idea what exactly I found, I know that it was something painful enough to be broken apart and entombed in the backyard across the street, but something precious enough to keep close.

* * *

The next morning, things are quiet in the kitchen, and that's when I know something's up.

Normally, Dad is slamming pots and pans around and asking Mom where the cumin is or how we could have possibly used the last of the olive oil, and Mom is trying to talk to him about sodium bicarbonate or how some student had to use the eye flusher in class.

Today, though, I don't hear any of that from the landing at the top of the stairs. Instead, I hear quiet murmuring.

"But what would be the point of that?"

"I haven't got a clue. A prank?"

"To prove what, exactly?"

"That . . . mannequins exist?"

"Yes, Jay. I'm certain someone is desperate to spread the good word about mannequins."

The mention of mannequins makes my stomach twist as I descend the stairs and try to decipher their whispered code.

"Apparently, they disabled the security system, but they didn't take anything. How bizarre is that?"

When I appear in the kitchen, they both look surprised to see me, which is weird because I live here.

"What's going on?" I ask, not really wanting to know, but wanting to get the guessing over with.

"The natural grocer had a break-in," Mom says, never one to tiptoe around an answer.

"Oh," I say. I know I should say "That's awful" or "How could someone do that?" but I'm not exactly in a position to be judgy, given my history of pranking the place with Aaron, using an intricately made fart synthesizer of my own design, and, well, *farts*.

RAVEN ✹ BROOKS ✹ BANNER

Fresh Prank Rattles Tillman's Natural Grocer

No suspect yet in odd case; owner disturbed by strange mannequin

"I wonder if it was the llama guy," Dad says, and Mom gives him a tired look.

"What? They have beef, you know. Something going way back to when she used to sell cheese from his goats."

Mention of Farmer Llama threatens to tip me over the edge, and I have to sit down so my parents can't see my legs shaking.

"What were you saying about a, er, mannequin?" I ask in the least convincing casual voice ever.

Mom shrugs. "Someone put a mannequin in the natural grocer."

Dad isn't satisfied with her answer, though. The man can sniff out a story from a mile away. He's like a gossip bloodhound. It must be a side effect of working in the news for so long.

"They *posed* a mannequin in there," he says. "In the second-floor office, just sitting in a chair."

Dad is downright giddy, but I can't bring myself to look him in the eyes. He'll know I'm hiding something. I don't have to try too hard because he turns his attention back to Mom, desperate to get her as amped as he is about this new development in the weird, weird town of Raven Brooks.

"I hear it didn't have a face. It was just . . . blank. How creepy is that?"

I choke on the water I didn't even want to drink in the first place.

"See?" Dad says. "Narf thinks it's creepy."

No, Narf doesn't think it's creepy. Narf thinks it's ABSOLUTELY INSANE how no one seems to remember that Mr. Peterson dug up a mannequin in the park last winter that sounds awfully similar to the one my parents are describing so casually.

"I'm going over to Enzo's," I say, standing up so suddenly I nearly knock my chair over.

My parents look at me, puzzled.

"Engineering club business," I say, and that's all it takes for them to stop worrying. I'm doing normal kid stuff. I'm definitely not planning to find a way into Mrs. Tillman's store to see the mannequin for myself.

"You might want to wear daytime clothes," Dad says. "I hear that's what the kids are doing these days."

I look down at my pajama'd self and nod, disappointing Dad by not laughing at his second joke of the morning. I chuckle to try to appease him, but it comes too late. He's suspicious again.

"We decided on a name. Engineering Masters of the Universe," I say.

"EMU," Dad says, and I knew he'd get it right away. "Solid name."

He may not be fully convinced that I'm fine, but that should buy me another day. Just enough to find out what the Aliens is going on over at the natural grocer.

* * *

I'm having déjà vu standing here in front of the natural grocer, trying to figure out a way in.

"I don't know why, but for some reason, I wasn't expecting crime scene tape," Trinity says. She was already over at Enzo and Maritza's house when I arrived at their doorstep, breathless and urgent. Enzo was like me; he had to see it for himself. Trinity, ever practical, warned us about this very scenario—that we wouldn't be able to get close enough to take a look.

Maritza, as usual, kept quiet around me. Well, as usual *lately*. I'm sure I was imagining it, but I swear I felt her eyes burning a hole through my back the entire walk to the store.

"I mean, a crime was technically committed," Enzo offers.

"Yeah, but it's sort of a pointless crime, isn't it? I mean, who breaks into a place to leave something there. And something so . . . *weird*?" Trinity says, but we all grow quiet because we know it isn't that weird. We've seen a strange, faceless mannequin before, just like the one my dad described over breakfast. I just need to know if it's the same one.

If it is, there's no denying, at least to Enzo and Maritza and Trinity, that Mr. Peterson is up to something. He's the only one in possession of one of those faceless creepers last I checked.

"All right, so how do we get in?" Enzo asks, and I am surprised that I've never noticed something about him before. He's . . . *good.* It's never even occurred to him to pick a lock or to sneak in through a back door. I suddenly feel like the world's worst influence. I don't think this is what my parents had in mind when they encouraged me to use my powers for good.

"Nicky should know how," Maritza says, the first time she's spoken all morning. And I feel the sting of those four words as sharply as she intended for me to feel them. It's hard for me to argue with her, though. I'm already sliding the lockpick set from my back pocket, opening it for the first time in a long while. The last time I used them—picking the lock on the Peterson house—feels like ages ago.

The sun beats down on the back of my neck as I assess the lock and choose the right pick for the job. I steady my hands, and there's that déjà vu feeling again because it should be Aaron looking over my shoulder while I'm doing this, not Enzo and Trinity.

Maritza's wandered away, though, and I don't know where to until she says, "Didn't there used to be a Missing poster here?"

I turn and see her standing by the light post stationed at the corner of the grocer's parking lot. All that remains on the post is a piece of duct tape clinging to the torn edge of a piece of paper.

"Yeah," Trinity says. "It's crazy. I thought there were at least five or so posted all over the Square, but last time I was there, I couldn't find a single one. Who would tear those down? That just seems—"

"Wrong. It's just wrong," Maritza says sharply, and why do I feel like that assessment was aimed at me? Maybe because she's LOOKING RIGHT AT ME.

"I'm starting to get nervous, Nicky. I don't know that this is such a good idea," Enzo says, saving us from one awkward moment just to move us into another.

"You don't have to do this with me," I say, and it comes out a little more wounded than I wanted it to.

I'm trying to look at Enzo, but the sun is glaring off the concrete, and all I can see are black spots where my eyes can't focus. Just then, one of the spots across Main Street in the distance appears to form the shape of a person, and because my brain is clearly broken, I swear I see the unmistakable outlines of a curled handlebar mustache at the top of that shape.

I cover my eyes with my hand, rubbing my eyeballs until the shapes disappear, then squint again into the distance.

Nothing.

"No, it's okay," Enzo says.

"Huh?" I answer, still distracted by what I thought I saw.

"I said it's okay. I'll go," Enzo says, and now I feel even worse because I know he's just trying to be brave, and I want so badly to tell him I'm completely terrified, but this lock is way too easy to pick, like it's already been loosened for me somehow, and before I can say another word, the handle to the back door of the natural grocer turns in my hand, and we're inside an official crime scene.

The lights are all out, and I'm fighting back the panic that begins to creep in because those shelves with their shadowy contents feel way too familiar.

This isn't your nightmare, I tell myself. *This isn't your nightmare.*

I squeeze my eyes closed for a minute and wait for the grocery store shelves in my mind to shrink from towering to the height of my head, and when I open my eyes, my nightmare fades to the background.

"Does anyone know where it is?" Trinity whispers, even though we're the only ones here.

"Upstairs," I say, indicating the staircase in the back corner of the store.

"How do you know that?" Maritza asks, and there's another accusation.

"My dad said it was at her desk," I say defensively. "Her desk was by the sound system Aaron and I messed with—upstairs."

She doesn't look convinced, but I don't have time to convince her. The longer we spend in here, the greater our chances of getting caught. A third meeting with Officer Keith is *not* what I want to write about in my "How I Spent My Summer Vacation" essay.

I lead the train of criminals under another strip of crime scene tape, and when I reach the top of the stairs, I carefully peel the secure tape from the door, taking a deep breath before swinging the door open.

Mrs. Tillman's desk is cluttered with paperwork—piles of invoices and manifests, wires from her never-repaired sound system, a random green tennis ball.

And there in the rolling office chair beside the desk sits a rigid form, the back of its head blank and pale.

I hear a clicking behind me and realize it's the sound of Trinity swallowing the air into her lungs.

The mannequin's back is to us, hiding the full extent of its presence, as though it could go unnoticed.

I take two steps forward on legs I can't feel, pulling my arm from Trinity's grasp, which wasn't holding me too tightly anyway because she might be trying to protect me from what I'm about to see, but she needs to see it as badly as I do. We all need to see it.

I reach a trembling hand out to the back of the chair and pull in a shaking breath before spinning the chair around and taking one giant step back, putting as much space between it and myself as possible.

Dad was wrong. Its face isn't blank. It would be so much better if it were blank.

Instead, someone has drawn a crude set of wide, unblinking eyes onto its surface. When people talk about being scared to death, this is what I imagine their corpse would look like, frozen in terror, rigid and permanent, its last moments petrified.

And below those wide, horrified eyes, that same person has adhered two strips of black electrical tape in the shape of an X, just over where the mouth of this grotesque figure should be.

"I don't want to do this anymore," Maritza says, breaking from the group and thundering down the stairs, unworried by the noise she makes as she flees the scene. Trinity follows without a word, and Enzo utters, "C'mon," without turning to see if I follow.

In silent agreement, we all run. We run as fast as our feet can carry us, away from the mannequin with the wide, searching eyes and the dark store and the picked lock, until the heat of the midday sun takes its toll and we have to stop.

We pant and wipe sweat from our brows, and each of us waits for the other to speak first. It turns out to be me, and I regret it almost instantly.

"Who would do that?"

"As if you don't know," Maritza says, like acid.

"Mari," Trinity tries to calm her, but it's no use.

"Oh please, we're all thinking it. I'm just the only one willing to say it."

Then she turns to me, her gaze cutting right through me.

"We know it was you, Nicky. You can drop the act because it's getting boring."

She doesn't look bored, though. She looks like she wants to rotate me on a spit over a roaring flame.

I look from Enzo to Trinity and wait for one of them to tell me that's not true, that her even suggesting it is crazy, but something on the sidewalk must be fascinating because they're just staring at it, refusing to look up.

"You all think that? You think *I* put that mannequin in there?"

"Nah, I don't believe it," Enzo says, way too late to be convincing.

I look to Trinity. "And you? Even after what you saw last night in Aaron's window?" I'm suddenly not so hot anymore. I feel a chill traveling through every single vein in my body.

"I mean, think about it, Nicky. What did we really see? Just a bunch of flashing lights," Trinity says, and I can hardly believe what I'm hearing.

Except I can. Because what made me think I could have a normal life in a normal town like some normal kid who plays sports on the weekend and puts off his homework until the last minute and has normal arguments with his parents about normal things like grades and curfews?

"Maybe we just need to keep away from all of it, you know? Like we told our parents we would," Enzo offers, and I guess I should be grateful that at least he hasn't completely turned his back on me, too.

"How could you all think—?" I begin. Those mannequins are *heavy*. I wouldn't know from lifting one, but seeing Mr. Peterson try to pry one from the dirt, seeing the way they moved around the ride in Spree Land . . . they don't look like something I would be capable of picking up off the ground for a second, let alone hauling it to the center of Main Street and up a flight of stairs just to pose for my own amusement.

Then, suddenly, all the anger rushes back to me. "So then what do you all think my master plan was here?"

"We're trying to be good friends, Nicky—" Trinity begins.

I can't think of a single thing to say, certainly nothing that would change any of their minds at this point. Not when they're this convinced that I'm some crazy mastermind.

"Whatever," I say, and it's so lame. I sound like a pouting toddler. I want to scream at them that they're kidding themselves. I want to take them by the shoulders and shake the sense back into them, to push away all the denial that's making them hide from the ridiculously obvious fact that Mr. Peterson is behind all of this weirdness. I have no idea why he's doing all of it, but that's no reason to doubt that he is.

That's no reason to doubt *me*.

I turn my back on my friends the way they've turned their backs on me. I walk home without even remembering how I got there. I roast under the sun and let it burn my neck. I drip with sweat and let it soak my shirt.

I go to my room and ignore the five calls Enzo tries to make, ducking every question my mom asks in her worried voice. I stare at the ceiling and wonder when the time will come that we'll leave Raven Brooks behind, and I'll start over in yet another town.

Next time, I won't even bother to make friends.

Chapter 4

I'm dreaming. I know because Aaron is there.

But the back of Aaron's head is all I see. My body may have let me claim a couple of hours of rest, but my mind can't sit still.

He's seated at his bedroom desk, his arm moving in short bursts. Something is scratching on the wood, and the sound is deafening in an otherwise empty room.

"This is what I do to escape," he says, refusing to turn around.

"What do you mean? I can't see what you're doing," I say.

He keeps scratching.

"To escape what?" I ask.

He doesn't answer.

"Why won't anyone believe me that you're not gone?"

The scratching quiets, but he still won't turn around. He still won't answer me.

"Aaron, where are you?"

Finally, he does answer.

"I'm right here," he says. "I've always been right here."

"But why can't I find you?" I ask.

The scratching resumes, and suddenly, it hurts my ears so badly, I crouch to the ground and press my arms to my head.

"Aaron!" I yell, but he can't hear me anymore. Or he's stopped listening.

The room begins to brighten to a light so white, it blinds me. Just before I lose sight of him completely, I hear his faint voice over the scratching:

"You're not going to like where this path ends, Nicky. Take it from me. You're going to wind up lost, unless—"

The blinding light from my dream is suddenly accompanied by the rumble and buzz of a lawn mower, and I open my eyes to the brightest sun that's ever tried to burn through my eyeballs.

The curtain over my window doesn't stand a chance against the sun of a Raven Brooks summer.

I fumble around on my bedside table for the alarm clock and can't believe it's already nine thirty in the morning.

"I guess heightened paranoia really takes it out of a person," I say.

I rub my eyes to try to rid myself of the images from my dream—Aaron hunched over his desk, the scratching, his unfinished warning that sounded way too much like my grandma's to bring me any sense of comfort.

I press my forehead to the window and look for the lawn mower culprit and am dismayed to find it's my own dad.

"Seriously?" I ask him through the window, but there's not a chance he knows I exist right now. He has his headphones on, and I'd bet an entire box of Twinkies that he's jamming out to the Grateful Dead. The man is a certified Deadhead. Mom has never given me a straight answer on the topic, but I'm 98 percent sure he followed them on tour for a chunk of time during his college years. For as long as I can remember, there's been a tie-dyed teddy bear sticker on the back of our car, the only sticker that's always had a place beside the license plates that have changed with every new state we've called home.

I'm just beginning to adjust to the sun's glare, when a small movement from the corner of my eye captures my attention.

I press my head a little harder to the window and scan the yard for the movement. It only takes me a second to find that there's a little yellow paper wedged into the vines climbing up the trellis underneath my window.

I look up at my dad and find him on the other side of the yard now, pushing his head forward and backward in a steady rhythm to whatever's playing through his headphones. He's steering the mower toward the trellis now, and I look nervously to the note that's flapping harder, disturbed by the gusts of air that the nearby motor is kicking up.

"No, Dad, back away. Back away!" I shout, banging on the glass, but even without the mower running, and even without the headphones playing, I'm still yelling at him through a closed window.

I could run downstairs. I could pull the extension cord.

Nope, no time. He'll be at the trellis in just a few seconds.

Instead, I hold my breath as he inches toward the vines, wholly unaware of the destruction he's about to unleash. I want to close my eyes, but I can't seem to turn away.

Then, just as the paper looks like it's about to dislodge and succumb to the spinning blade, Dad pulls back on the handle and turns off the engine, stooping to empty the basket into the green bin before returning to the scene. Then, to my relief, he pushes the mower a couple of paces in the other direction before turning the engine on and starting his next column with his back to me.

Now's my chance.

I slide the window open and pop the screen out of its frame before easing myself onto the first rung of the trellis, feeling the usual give on the slat before lowering the rest of my body onto the makeshift ladder I've grown accustomed to using to sneak out of my room.

The wood groans a little louder than usual, and I can feel at least one of the steps splintering under my weight.

"Just keep it together this one time, and I promise I'll never use you again," I tell the trellis, and I swear it stops splintering.

I peer over my shoulder at my dad, but his back is still to me as he bops along to a beat I can't hear.

I take a few more steps down and lower my hand to reach for the note, but my fingertips only barely graze the paper.

Just a few more inches.

I stretch until I think my shoulder will dislocate.

Curse my abnormally short arms!

I look up and see that Dad is just about at the edge of the driveway, which means he'll turn around in three . . .

C'mon, c'mon!

Two . . .

Almost there!

One.

Gotcha!

I snatch the note and scurry up the trellis just in time to swing my leg over the windowsill and duck under the frame.

I risk a peek into the yard to see if Dad's looking up here, but he's just mowing along like he didn't just come inches from obliterating a piece of possible evidence.

I take care to place the screen back in the window and slide it shut before turning my attention to the paper. I can see that whatever it is, it's written in thick red marker, just like the very first note Aaron smacked against his own window behind the glow of the flashlight.

I take a deep breath and unfold the sheet of paper.

It's two words, and they mean nothing.

"What?"

It feels like a joke, like someone must be pulling the world's most elaborate gag, and somewhere, they're ducked behind their own window, laughing hysterically as they watch me dangle from my rickety trellis and grasp at clues to find the only friends who never turned their backs on me.

I read the note over and over, hoping the words will change, hoping they'll make some sort of sense, but there's nothing to it. Just those two words and a little black smudge in the shape of a thumb.

How could it be that the other night the signals from across the street were so clear, and today it's like someone just wrote two random words on a piece of paper and left them in a random bush for some random kid to pick up and obsess over?

* * *

The note bothers me all morning, well into getting dressed and willing myself to face my friends. But I can't take my mind off the message—I try anagramming the letters to spell something else, try writing it out in Morse code. Nothing. It's killing me to the extent that I can't concentrate on anything EMU-related, which was the entire point of meeting up with everyone today. Well, that and pretending like the last time we all got together didn't end super awkward.

"And then we'll put Nicky in charge of the hamster rodeo," Enzo says.

"Right, okay," I say absently.

"Dude, wake up," Enzo says, snapping his fingers in front of my face.

"What? I said I'd do it!" I say defensively.

They all wait for me to realize I've completely checked out of the conversation.

"What's the matter with you today?" Enzo asks, giving up on EMU planning for now.

Maybe it's the lack of sleep or the fact that we actually had a decent time EMU planning today and things are almost starting to feel normal again. Maybe the heat is just wearing me down. Whatever the case, I blurt it out.

"Something weird happened this morning," I say, and I hear three chairs around me creak as they all shift in their seats.

"Weird like hamster-rodeo weird, or weird like that bat that only has one and a half wings that flies around the neighborhood?" Enzo asks.

"I've seen that bat," Maritza says, speaking up for the first time the whole afternoon. "I feel sorry for it."

I shake off the bat talk. "Weird like a note. It was stuck in the bushes under my window."

"Oh man, Nicky," Enzo says, shaking his head and looking tired. Like he's got anything to be tired about.

"I know it sounds crazy, but I think it might be Aar—"

"You're right, it *does* sound crazy," Maritza says, and there it is—she sounds angry with me again. She still believes I was behind the mannequin at the natural grocer. She won't look at me, either, and now Enzo's the only one who doesn't seem to be afraid to make eye contact. What is going on here?

"I think it was Aaron," I say, pushing my luck. "Maybe Mya. They've both left me notes there before."

I wait for one of them to say something. To say anything.

"It said 'red key,'" I say, flailing for whatever will get them to answer me. "What does that even mean, 'red key'?"

Enzo and Trinity shake their heads, clearly as lost as I am, even if they aren't quite as worked up as me. Not Maritza, though. She's looking right at me now. She's trying to cut a hole through me with her eyes. Again.

"Nicky . . ." Trinity says, sighing. "We're supposed to be letting this go, remember?"

"Right, and I was," I say. "But how am I supposed to ignore what's happening across the street from me? And this morning—you guys, the note was *in my yard*!"

"Why are you so obsessed?" Enzo asks flatly.

"Why *aren't* you?" I shoot back. "If that was Aaron in the window the other night—"

Trinity steps in. "Then this is still too big for us, Nicky. You remember that night in Farmer Llama's shed? He came *after* us. The parents are right—we did everything we could. Now we need to stay away—the guy is *unhinged*."

Enzo nods in agreement, and Maritza sits there hating me quietly, and I've never felt so abandoned.

"What if it were one of us?" I plead. "Wouldn't you want *someone* trying to find you?"

Three pairs of eyes suddenly drop to the table.

"You know what?" I say. "Forget it. Forget I said anything. In fact, forget I ever left my house at all today. It's like you never saw me."

I stand to leave.

"Nicky, don't be that way," Trinity says, but she's not exactly trying hard to get me to stay.

"Right," I say as I back out. "You're right. I won't be that way. I won't be any way. I'm just going to pretend everything's okay. After all, I'm making this whole thing up, right? I lugged a two-hundred-pound mannequin half-way across town by myself and I planted a note in my trellis, and, hey, maybe I rigged some robots in Aaron's bedroom to flash those lights we saw. You're right. It's all good, guys—it's just in my head."

We're all on the sidewalk, our drama having spilled outside.

"We're quitting EMU," Maritza blurts, and for a second, I forget about my hurt feelings and lost friends and flashing lights. All eyes are on Maritza now. I take a few steps back toward the group.

"Wait, what?"

"Yeah, what're you talking about?" Enzo says, and thank the Aliens I'm not the only one in the dark. He's just as surprised as I am.

Trinity looks at Maritza: "Maybe this isn't the best time."

"It's not like it's gonna get any less awkward," Maritza says.

"Why do you want to quit?" Enzo asks, wounded.

"Maybe not quit exactly," Trinity tries. "Maybe we just . . . er . . . reimagine the current mission of the club. So it's more in line with *all* of our interests."

"We don't want to play with robots," Maritza says, and Trinity interrupts.

"What Maritza means is we're a little more drawn to innovations that involve . . . um . . . a focus on social justice. Like what my parents do."

"She means we want to work with actual human beings," Maritza says to Enzo.

Enzo ignores her and turns to me. "Did you know about this?"

I glare at him. "Is that a serious question?"

I'm rolling my eyes, which is maybe why they're playing tricks on me, because all of a sudden, way down at the end of the street, a figure too far and too dark slides out from behind a fence.

The figure is tall, or maybe not, but from this distance, he looks tall. And his shadow fills the asphalt in front of him.

He stands, facing us, hands at his side. He stands and stares.

I blink hard a few times, sure I must be imagining anyone there at all. A more paranoid mind might think it was Mr. Peterson from the way his broad shoulders hulked. But that's ridiculous. And besides, whoever it was, he's gone now.

"So great," Enzo says to Trinity and Maritza, their conversation pulling me back in. "You're going to start your own club. Fine." He's doing a terrible job of playing it cool. "I mean, good luck getting sponsorship. We're already planning on approaching EarthPro for that, so . . ."

"Why couldn't we also approach EarthPro?" Maritza challenges, and she and Trinity wait for a good answer.

They might be waiting awhile.

"Because—because you know they're the only ones we can ask!" Enzo says.

He's not wrong. We've talked about it before. A nonschool entity has to back any new club that forms, serving as an official sponsor for their activities. But between our collective connections to the newspaper, the college, and every other local business owner I've ticked off by pranking, we're pretty much left with one option: EarthPro. Everyone else would be a conflict of interest or just . . . a conflict.

"Look, EarthPro is the only company that it actually makes sense for us to ask. I mean, they have a whole department called Community Connections," Trinity says, her trademark diplomacy grating on me because who cares about logic right now? They're basically threatening to torpedo EMU. It's EMU-icide. Suddenly, this club I didn't care too much about a few days ago is the most important thing in the world to me. Maybe because it's my last actual connection to the normal moving-on kind of life I'm supposed to be living.

"So, let's each pitch our club to them," Enzo says, looking to me for support, but that's just a terrible idea.

"Great idea," Trinity says.

No. It's terrible.

"Fine," Enzo says.

"Fine," Trinity says.

Terrible.

The four of us part ways, a false armistice reached, and I've almost forgotten how hurt I was over the fact that no one would believe me about Aaron and the note.

Almost, that is, until I make it all the way to the end of the street and turn around. They're all walking home together. I'm the only one walking alone.

When I get home, I don't feel like going in. I can't face the inquisition yet, with Mom asking if we got some good work done like we have jobs or something while Dad makes more bird jokes. Instead, I sit in the backyard and pull the grass up in clumps for no good reason. Maybe it just feels good to have power over something.

I'm right next to the back porch, which is the only reason I see the canvas bag stashed underneath it. It's not that I forgot about the bag so much as I forgot how much I was trying to avoid it. I'm still not sure why it was buried in the first place, why the tapes were broken.

But seeing the bag cast out of sight like that suddenly makes me feel sorry for it. What did those tapes ever do to deserve that broken and buried fate? With a chill, I suddenly remember another tape that succumbed to the same fate as those, a certain *Tooth* VHS with a new surprise ending featuring a certain neighbor losing his marbles while the rest of his family watched.

I can't believe it's taken me this long to remember the similarities. Did the same person break those tapes in the bag? Did they feature more of the same horrors from the Peterson house? Did they show something even worse?

Are the pieces of the *Tooth* video in that bag?

I wait the day away until my parents have retired to their separate corners for the evening, distracted by work or TV, and sneak in through the back door, the bag slung over my shoulder.

"Narf, that you?" Dad calls from his office.

"Went great, Dad! Great EMU progress. Everything's awesome!" I call over my shoulder as I head upstairs.

"Nicky, have you eaten dinner?" Mom yells from behind a stack of papers in her room.

"Couldn't be better, Mom! Lots of normal kid fun. Engineering and stuff!" I say before closing my bedroom door.

In my room, I look for an adequate hiding spot until I can figure out what to do with the tapes.

"Narf, hide the evidence; I'm coming in," Dad says, and I hear his footsteps pad down the hallway.

Sometimes Dad's jokes feel eerily prophetic.

I throw the bag into the deepest corner of my closet without looking and race to my bed, throwing the covers over me and putting on my best I-was-just-drifting-off-to-sleep look.

"What's going on?" I ask, pretending to be groggy as Dad pops his head in.

"Oops, sorry, Narf," he says. "Didn't realize you were . . ."

He looks at his watch, puzzled.

"A little early for bed, isn't it?"

"Dad," I say, and only one excuse comes to mind. "I'm a teenager."

"Say no more," Dad says, and flicks off the light before retreating to the hallway. It's the newest excuse for strange behavior. It's like the perfect, mystical answer that means nothing but somehow still works. Magic.

It takes about another century for the telltale snores to waft from my parents' room.

When I finally hear them, I creep out of bed, still in my day clothes, and retrieve the bag from its sad excuse for a hiding place. It's left clumps of dirt and grass all over my closet, but I'll deal with that later.

Right now, all I care about is getting a better look at those tapes. Upon unzipping the bag, I see that they're actually in worse shape than I'd first realized. The celluloid is knotted into massive clumps and mounds, except for when it's been completely torn apart. The reels are still somewhat intact, but the cases are in shambles, with jagged edges forming pieces of the world's weirdest puzzle. Whoever hid these tapes didn't just destroy them; they tried to demolish them.

Not all was lost, though. Because there in the shadowy folds of the filthy canvas bag with its broken memories is a yellowed sticker label, the handwriting faint but instantly familiar.

Only the "Too" remains before the rest of the word is torn away, its other pieces likely buried in the rest of these fractured parts. But there's no doubt in my mind that the *Tooth* video—the one that captured just a sliver of the madness across the street—resides in this bag of hidden memories I absolutely was not supposed to find.

Chapter 5

For the first time in my life, I don't want to play video games.

I'm only sitting in Enzo's game room because by the sixth call from him, Mom had decided that whatever it was, we could work it out.

Actually, her exact words were "I'm not your secretary, and this isn't your office, so find someplace else to work on your sullen adolescence."

Apparently, she and Dad had planned a romantic night in, which grossed me out just enough to make me put on my shoes and hear Enzo's plan to re-form EMU, not that anything he said was going to make a difference after Nigiri Nights.

Of the three of them, at least Enzo still feels like he's sort of on my side. Not that you'd know it from the way he keeps trying to steer the conversation.

"It's because of what happened at Spree Land," he says while I throttle him with my tiny alligator arms.

"I told you The Finch has a weak spot. You can't punch with a wing," I say, completely ignoring anything other than *Manimal Maul*. Just because I'm annoyed with him doesn't mean I have to deprive myself of the newest, greatest beat-'em-up video game.

"It freaked her out. Maritza's not going to tell you that, but it bothered her. She won't even tell *me* why, and that's saying something because usually I can't get her to shut up."

"You're going down, bird man. This is about to get ugly. Like, man-bird-hybrid ugly," I say, stealing the last of his life force with my freakishly strong miniature hands.

"I don't get why he doesn't just bite everyone," Enzo says, and he's not wrong.

"Maybe that's a cheat code or something," I say, resetting the game for another round, but Enzo puts his controller down.

"What? I'll let you be Swamper this time," I say, but we both know I didn't come over to play *Manimal Maul*. I came over so Enzo could convince me to smooth things over with Maritza. It's not just about EMU; it's about all the weirdness going on between us even before the girls dropped the bomb that they wanted their own club.

And while Enzo's busy defending Maritza, he's conveniently leaving out the part where he and Trinity grew suddenly mute when she was accusing me of planting the mannequin.

"She seems angry, but that's how Maritza acts when she's scared," Enzo says.

"See, that's strange," I say. "Because when I'm scared, I act . . . oh golly, what's the word? *Scared*," I say.

Okay, so maybe when I'm scared, I act sarcastic. But I can't exactly tell him that I'm afraid of losing all my friends because they think I'm off my nut. How do you convince someone you're not losing your marbles without sounding like you're losing your marbles?

"Look, just meet up with her for sushi tonight. I'll find a reason Trinity and I can't go. Don't leave until she tells you what's wrong. Just . . . figure it out."

I stare at him, looking for all the reasons to say no, but it occurs to me that maybe he's not doing this for me. Maybe he's doing this for him. He's worried about his sister, and so far, he hasn't been successful in getting her to talk.

* * *

Five hours later, I'm ordering my third refill of soda and checking my own watch obsessively while Maritza runs twenty minutes late.

I've just decided that this was the world's worst idea, when she comes stumbling through the front door, and I know I'm a tad paranoid these days, but I'd swear I see Trinity's hand at her back right before the door swings shut, leaving Maritza looking abandoned.

She walks toward the table slowly and slides into the bench as far away from me as she can get while sitting at the same table.

"Is that really necessary?" I ask, already annoyed.

"I don't know, is it?" she says, which doesn't exactly qualify as a comeback. It doesn't really qualify as anything.

The waitress places a mug of tea in front of Maritza, and she eagerly takes a sip, even though it's probably hot enough to burn her tongue. She looks relieved to have something to do with her hands. I slurp the last of my watered-down soda and fight the urge to sprint to the bathroom. I have to pee desperately, but for some reason, it would seem like admitting defeat if I left the table right now.

Maritza sets down her mug a little too hard on the table, and we both jump when our chopsticks skitter like ants across the surface.

"I'm not crazy," she says, and I blink a couple of times, because that's all I can think to do.

Then, as though a hard shell has suddenly cracked, I see a glimmer of the old Maritza behind it, the Maritza who wasn't afraid of anything, who made me sweat for no good reason, whose dimple in the side of her chin is impossible to see unless you look really closely, which I totally haven't.

"I'm not crazy, either," I say, and there we have it. There's what's been slowly forming that shell around her all summer. All this time, she's been worried that I think she's crazy, and I've been worried that she thinks I'm crazy, and we were so busy being defensive, we forgot to ask what we were defending ourselves against.

Except for . . .

"Why would you think I think you're crazy?" I ask. Maritza's a whole lot of things: sharp-witted, wicked smart, funny . . . but crazy? Nope, that one was reserved for the likes of me, and maybe a neighbor who shall remain nameless.

Maritza starts to fidget in her chair.

"Why would you say I had something to do with the mannequin in Mrs. Tillman's store?" I ask, growing tired of guessing.

"It's just that . . . we all know you're having a hard time dropping this Mr. Peterson thing," she says, her eyes on the table, "and with all those Missing signs disappearing—"

"But that wasn't me—"

"—and thinking you saw the lights and everything—"

"Trinity saw those, too!" I say, and we both go quiet again.

"So, you guys have been thinking I'm responsible for all these things?" I ask. No, I demand.

"Actually, Trinity and Enzo thought I was the paranoid one at first," she says.

"At first," I say. Clearly, that opinion has shifted to someone else at this table. Someone who really, desperately has to pee now, but there's no chance I'm going to be the first one to walk away.

"What exactly is it you all think I'm deviously plotting, then? Oooh, I know. Do a bunch of weird, random stuff that makes me look nuts. That'll show them all I'm sane."

"No," she says, sounding annoyed, which annoys me even more. "We think . . ." Then she corrects herself, "*I* thought you were doing it to keep Mr. Peterson looking suspicious."

I put my hands up to stop her. "Hang on, hang on," I say, "You thought I was doing all this scheming and making all these elaborate plans, just so people would keep suspecting Mr. Peterson was behind Aaron's and Mya's disappearance?"

Maritza shrugs. "Well, everyone wants you to stop talking about it, so maybe you were trying to *show* people instead of getting them to try to listen to you. It just seems like something you'd do. You know, cuz you're smart and all," she says.

Suddenly, I'm hot. Like someone turned off the air-conditioning, and why am I sweating, and why is my face throbbing?

"But I'm also lazy," I say, and she lifts an eyebrow at me. "Do you honestly think I'd put in all that work over summer break?"

It only takes Maritza a second to show me the smile I figured I'd never see again. Seriously, it's like someone filled this place with wood-fire stoves. What is going on?

"No, there's no way you'd work that hard," she says.

Seeing her smile at me gives me an ounce of courage back, so I press my luck.

"So, you and Trinity are really going to leave EMU?" I say, and she squirms uncomfortably in her chair.

"I mean, it's not like EMU was an *actual* club yet anyway," she says.

"I thought you liked robots," I say. She starts to falter.

"I *do*. It's just . . . I want to be a good friend to Trinity, too, and she seems really excited about—"

"Responsible sourcing. Community engagement," I say, letting my head fall back in a deep, mock snore.

Maritza laughs. It's an actual, honest-to-Aliens laugh I haven't heard from her since Spree Land.

"It's not that ba—"

I snore louder. She laughs louder. It's glorious.

"Do you want to get tacos? I'm feeling kind of burned out on sushi," she says, and I can't get out of my chair fast enough.

"Let me just go to the bathroom first, before I damage an internal organ," I say, and I practically mow down the waitress on my way to the restroom.

Maritza is waiting outside, and maybe it's my blissfully empty bladder, but I feel lighter than I have all summer, which I guess is why I feel so comfortable unloading absolutely everything that's been on my mind for weeks.

"Where exactly did you think I would have gotten one of those creepy mannequins from?" I ask, and Maritza looks embarrassed.

"Maybe you have a stash of them in your room or something. I don't know what you do in your free time. Maybe you're making mannequin art installations."

"Yeah, that sounds like me," I say. "You found me out." I mockingly look at my watch. "Oh, it's seven o'clock! Time to go see Nicky's performative art show with the super-creepy mannequins! So glad I asked for all those art supplies for my birthday," I say, and I'm maybe ten steps ahead on the sidewalk when I realize I'm walking alone.

I turn to find Maritza staring off at something in the distance.

"The paper," she says. "I'd almost forgotten about the paper."

"What paper?" I ask, turning to look over my shoulder at whatever she's looking at. But when I turn back around, it's me Maritza is staring right at.

"The paper the ride operator found at Spree Land. The one that he found on your seat."

It feels like nighttime has come on all at once, and out of nowhere, I feel the first hint of a chill in the air. I don't think it has anything to do with the weather, though.

"Okaaaaay," I say, bracing myself for whatever revelation Maritza's had, because I have a sneaking suspicion that it has to do with me.

"How did you get that paper?" she asks, and her tone is so accusatory, I feel the defensiveness sneaking back in.

"What are you talking about? You know, for someone who doesn't want to come across as paranoid, you're doing a pretty bad job of convincing me you're not," I say.

Maritza takes a step toward me and holds my gaze. "That Missing poster. The art on the back of it looked like his art."

I try to sort through her accusations, but they're all tangled up.

The paper at Spree Land, the one the ride operator said was mine.

"Hang on, the Missing poster?" I say.

"They've been disappearing all over town. Don't tell me you haven't noticed," she says.

"Of course I've noticed. But, Maritza, c'mon. I thought you believed me," I plead, and I hate how desperate I sound, but why has she all of a sudden found a new reason to distrust me? What did she mean "*his* art"?

"Wait, you know who drew that picture on the back?"

She scoffs at me. "Like you don't."

"I *don't*!"

"I can't believe I didn't see it before," Maritza says, and she's stopped accusing me. She's already moved on. She's talking to herself, dismissing me completely. "What better way to make sure we keep suspecting Mr. Peterson than to make sure we find Aaron's art on the back of his own Missing poster."

Aaron's art?

She turns back to me, her eyes glittering wild with speculation. "I don't know how you did it, if you copied one of his pictures or whatever, but that's pretty messed up, Nicky."

Aaron's the artist. It was his makeshift gallery behind the factory. It was his sketches of people with their terrified faces trapped in their grotesque amusement park, crying out silently for help. It was his shadowy drawing on the back of that poster.

"Maritza, whatever you think you know, I can promise

you you're wrong," I say, still trying to process this new revelation.

"I don't know what's worse," she says, backing away from me. "The fact that you tore down the posters or the fact that you had his drawing."

"Maritza—"

"I'm out, Nicky. You're on your own. You've gone too far," she says, and with that, she turns and runs.

She runs away from me.

I picture myself going after her. I imagine running behind her all the way home, screaming between breaths that whatever she thinks I did, it wasn't me, it wasn't me, she has to believe me, it wasn't me.

I picture myself doing that, but I can't seem to move. Maybe it's because I can't figure out what it means that Aaron was the one drawing those horrifying pictures. Or that someone is still drawing those pictures—and of all places, on the backs of his Missing posters.

If Aaron's trying to tell me he's still here, why would he tear down the posters that might help to find him?

Chapter 6

n my dream, the back room of the grocery store is freezing, but it isn't as dark as it should be. It isn't as dark because there's a light flickering on and off, on and off.

It's coming from underneath one of the towering shelves, and I have to climb down from the grocery cart to see.

ClickClickClick. Click Click. ClickClickClick.
ClickClickClick. Click Click. ClickClickClick.

"Who's there?" I ask, standing in front of the flashing light now, the beam brightening my feet, then darkening them, brightening, then darkening.

"Who's doing that?"

I slowly crouch to my hands and knees and lower my head to the cold linoleum, sinking to eye level with whatever is under the shelf.

Matted gray hair parts to show me the wrinkled face of Bubbe Fein, her mouth drawn in a grin as she giggles uncontrollably. She flicks the light on and off and laughs at her game.

ClickClickClick. Click Click. ClickClickClick.

"Bubbe, stop," I tell her, but I can't find the words to tell her why. She's frightening me.

"Come play, Boychik. It's fun!"

But it isn't fun. I want to go home.

"I'm cold," I say.

My grandma stops smiling, and the beam of the flashlight rests just below her puckered chin, casting deep shadows across her face.

"So am I," she says, and suddenly, she begins to cry.

"I'm sorry, Bubbe. Don't cry," I plead, but she just wails and wails.

"I can't," she cries. "I can't stop. I told you, Nicky, I make bad things happen."

* * *

I wake with a gasp, sputtering for breath. My sheets are drenched in sweat, a by-product of the vivid nightmares I hoped I'd left behind.

I creep downstairs on shaking legs and pour myself a giant glass of water and drink it in a single breath before pouring myself another.

"It was just a dream," I tell myself, but how many times can I say that before I have to acknowledge that some of this is more than dreaming?

Some of this is *wandering*.

Bubbe Fein may have tried to teach me in all the wrong ways, but that doesn't mean what she was trying to teach me wasn't right.

Why else would I continue dreaming about her even after I learned what the grocery store dreams were about? After Mom told me what my grandma did—how she left me in that back room to teach me a lesson—shouldn't the dreams have stopped? Mystery solved, move on . . . right?

I'm still preoccupied with this question when I meet Enzo at his house the next morning. He's nervously tugging at the collar of his polo.

"All I'm saying is we need to be cool. We're lucky Ms. Delphine even said yes to a meeting," Enzo says as he walks a little too fast toward the shortcut through the woods.

"Is this you being cool?" I ask, dragging my feet because I didn't sleep well, and I know that's not Enzo's fault, but he's acting like we're interviewing for a job with NASA.

"What I mean is we can't afford to blow this," he says, his breath coming out in short huffs as we cut a path toward the old Golden Apple Amusement Park. "This might be our only chance to make a good impression on EarthPro."

Translation: If we botch this, we might as well introduce Trinity and Maritza to Ms. Delphine ourselves.

VISITOR BADGE
EarthPro Construction
Site Volunteer

Ms. Delphine greets us with a wide smile shaded by the brim of her hard hat. It looks weirdly out of place against her prim suit and heeled shoes.

"You must be Nicholas and Enzo," she says, shaking our hands in the wrong order of our names and handing us visitor badges and hard hats of our own.

"Nicky, hi," I say, giving her a little wave to indicate which one I am, but she has already turned around and begun walking.

Enzo and I shrug, don our hard hats, and follow her toward the remnants of the Golden Apple Amusement Park. As always, I do my best to conceal a shudder as I pass by the wreckage, but that's a task that's only grown tougher with each new horror that seems to emerge from its ashes.

The park used to belong to the forest. With the overgrowth weaving through the rusted carcasses of rides, it looked somehow alive. Or rather, undead. The vines had given the spokes and poles artificial life, the moldy leaves a sense of breath, albeit rotten breath. The park was rarely permeated by light, no matter how high the sun shone over it.

But now the vegetation has been cleared. The rides, once sparkling new, later frighteningly reanimated, now look somehow naked. Almost vulnerable. The sunlight that blankets the smooth dirt ground stands ready for cranes and demolition equipment to haul away the last of its charred and warped remains.

And a new foundation waits in the wings, ready to be poured over whatever secrets still lay buried in the park's grave.

"You boys have a very important job to do today," Ms. Delphine says, her voice oozing with sweetness.

"That's great!" Enzo says, matching her enthusiasm. "We actually have a few notes we'd like to share with you, too."

Recognizing my cue, I unshoulder my backpack and pull out a crisp folder with the carefully printed documents we toiled over in the week leading up to this meeting.

"We, uh, we've developed a vision and a mission statement for the club that we think could be pretty great for recruiting . . ."

But the more Enzo talks, the faster Ms. Delphine seems to walk, her black pumps kicking up small tufts of dust as she dodges

VISION

Our vision for this club is that it will be a place for people interested in engineering to get together and talk about our common interests. We'll discuss developments in engineering, new construction projects in the tri-county area, and finally, do a construction project of our own. We also plan to have real engineers visit to talk about what they do and how they decided to become an engineer.

EMU –
EarthPro Meeting

uneven ground and leads us past the park and toward the factory.

"Mm-hmm," she says, but her tone betrays not the slightest bit of interest in our vision or mission statement or need for the recruitment that will bring our club member number up to the critical point of receiving school approval. In fact, from what I can tell, all Ms. Delphine seems to be interested in is keeping her hard hat from sliding off her carefully styled hair.

"We could, uh, maybe save that for the next meeting if it's better—" I offer.

"I'm just so glad you boys are here," she says, and at least she's acknowledging us because for a second I wondered if we were phantoms following her around the Golden Apple ghost town.

"Great!" Enzo says, but I'm already suspicious. Ms. Delphine has her hands clasped in front of her like she's getting ready to start a cheer.

"You are going to help us with the re*engineering* of the space in the factory!" she says.

"I see what you did there," I say, "using the word 'engineering.'"

I think I see Ms. Delphine's smile slip for a second before she catches it and slaps it back on her face.

"So . . . more like a structural engineering kind of exercise?" Enzo tries, and Aliens bless my friend for wanting to believe that this isn't what I think it's going to be.

"Yes! That's very good. *Very* good," Ms. Delphine says. She's talking to Enzo like he's a three-year-old.

"What we need is for the EMU team," she says, making us sound very, *very* important, "to inventory and oversee the asset removal process of this entire property ahead of EarthPro's groundbreaking day!" She parts her arms like she's giving us the whole wide world.

"That—that sounds . . . good?" Enzo says, and hope has left his voice.

"Groundbreaking day?" I ask.

"Oh, I'm sure you kids have heard the news . . ."

We stare at her blankly.

"No? We're holding a big celebration for the town before we break ground on the new development. I'll make sure you kids get a flyer before you leave."

"Yes," I say. "Good. *Great.*"

Ms. Delphine searches our faces for sarcasm before blinking the dust out of her eyes.

"I'll go get you some goggles and respiratory masks, too. Lots of dust in there." She turns to walk away before calling over her shoulder, "By the way—I've convinced the company to donate some of the old parts to your little club. Should be some good odds and ends in there for constructing your own doodads! We've been lugging all sorts of junk from around the park to this outbuilding."

As soon as the factory door closes behind her and we can no longer hear the click of her heels, Enzo turns to me, his face sunken.

"Did she just tell us to—"

"Clean the factory. Yes."

"Is there any possible way this could be engineering-related?" he asks. He's begging for a hint of redemption to this day.

"Not unless you count me reengineering my attitude from bored to extremely bored," I say. "But hey, at least we get hard hats!"

Indeed we do. And goggles, and respiratory masks. And with a wave of her fingers, Ms. Delphine has left us to "reengineer."

We decide to start with the main factory floor: the area that used to house the conveyor belt that's since been removed. The space is for the most part empty, aside from some general debris that's accumulated over time along the edges of the floor.

"What do rat droppings look like?" Enzo calls to me from the far corner.

"I'm flattered you think I'd know," I say.

In fact, I would know, not that Enzo would realize that. Aaron would remember, though. I think back to the day he first showed me this factory, the one that used to be his secret, but that he shared with me. Because he trusted me. All of this was his, everything down to the rats and the poop they left like pebbles all over the ground. I don't hear their telltale skittering in the walls anymore.

"This can't be sanitary," Enzo says, moping even harder than me, if that's possible. "We need to ask for full oxygen masks next time, like *Mad Max*-style."

I'm hardly listening, though, because thinking about the rats reminds me of one of the last times I was in this place, and suddenly, all I can see flickering in front of me is the grainy footage of Mr. Peterson coming unraveled in front of an increasingly shadowed Aaron.

What was it Ms. Delphine said? That we could use some of the spare parts in the outbuilding?

"Of course, if we could just drop EarthPro as our EMU sponsor, maybe we could be doing actual work instead of making poop piles," Enzo says, jamming the bristles of his broom into the concrete.

If any of those spare parts included some of the video equipment that used to be in Aaron's and my "Office," maybe I could figure out a way to piece together the broken tapes and play them back.

"But we can't approach anyone else in town for sponsorship, can we?" Enzo grumbles right before he turns away to say under his breath, "Thanks for that, by the way."

"Huh?"

Enzo turns back around, his eyes wide with outrage. I know I should have been listening to him, but tapes feel a little more important right now.

"Enzo, I need to tell you something," I say, abandoning my broom and walking toward him. "I dug something up in Mr. Peterson's backyard."

I didn't think it was possible, but Enzo's eyes get even bigger.

"You did what in whose yard?!"

"I know, I know. But wait until you hear how weird it is. These tapes—well, they were tapes, but someone smashed them to bits—and they—"

"Are you completely insane?" Enzo says, and it's not a question.

"Enzo, listen to me. He buried them—"

"You haven't been listening to a word we've been saying," Enzo says, sounding more like my dad than . . . well, my dad, and that annoys me enough to sidetrack me from the tape talk.

"What're you going to do, ground me?" I say, and he just shakes his head like he's already given up on me.

"Look, can you just hear me out?" I say, trying to sound more diplomatic than I feel. "I think we might be able to use some of that old equipment to restore the videos."

Enzo stares at me. He blinks maybe once.

"Don't you get it? We might be able to use those to figure out what happened to Aaron and Mya!"

Another blink.

Then I say what it is I've wanted to say to all three of them all summer, what I've been trying to "move on" from.

"Don't you even care anymore?" Enzo takes a step back like I shoved him, even though I'm standing a good three feet away. His jaw is clenched, and I'm starting to wonder if maybe he's planning to shove *me*. Instead, he says, "Do you think it's easy constantly trying to convince everyone you're not a total lunatic?"

"Sorry it's such a burden being my friend," I say.

He suddenly looks so exhausted by me, and I know the feeling. Constantly defending myself is getting old.

"You're really starting to freak people out, you know that?" Enzo says. "Trinity and I sent you to Nigiri Nights so you could smooth things over with Maritza, but now she feels weirder than ever around you."

"If this is about that stupid paper—"

"It's not just the paper," he interjects. "It's what it means. If you had one of those Missing posters, then it's *you* who's been ripping them down."

"Why would I tear them down? They're the only thing left of Aaron and Mya. If you care so much about the Missing posters, why don't you help me *find them*?"

Enzo grows quiet. Then he lets loose the question he's clearly been harboring for a long time.

"It wasn't you, right? The dummy in Mrs. Tillman's store? And the paper at Spree Land, and the posters? Just say it wasn't you."

That he even has to ask, that despite everything I've said he still doesn't believe me, is what hurts the most.

"You're supposed to be my friend," I say.

"I *am* your friend. You're just making it really hard to believe you right now."

"Wow. I must be some master manipulator to have that sort of power over you. Maybe engineering's the wrong field for me. Maybe I should start a supervillains club."

"Knock it off," he says, but I'm not finished.

"Ooooh, we could figure out how to commit random, nonsensical crimes that will make everyone hate me and my friends all turn their backs on me. That's a *brilliant* idea."

"Nicky . . ." he says, but he has nothing else to say after that. Just a plea in the form of my name. It's like he can't be bothered to expend any more energy trying to believe me.

"Tell you what," I say. "You work on the whole EMU thing. I'll be upstairs plotting my next big move," I stomp up the stairs loud enough to make it echo through the cavernous factory.

I'm so busy huffing and stomping and basically making as much noise as humanly possible that, when I finally stop, I don't recognize the corridor I'm in.

I push away an unsettling flashback of getting lost in Aaron's house and instead try retracing my steps to find my way back. But I was so busy nursing my wounds, I wasn't paying any attention at all to my surroundings. It's another corridor like the longer one where Aaron and I set up the Office once upon a time, but this definitely isn't the same one. It's shorter, and all these doors stand open. They've probably been ransacked already, but given the last haul of parts I was able to take away from the factory, my instinct for spare parts overrides my anger for the moment.

The first three rooms yield nothing but some unintelligible graffiti and a random crumpled candy wrapper. One room looks out onto the train tracks and the old, abandoned weather station that mark the edge of Raven Brooks.

The fourth room, though, the fourth room is the jackpot.

This electronics graveyard isn't nearly as big as the other one; most of it is long, heavy cords and old breaker box switches, a rusted pair of wire cutters and a half-used roll of black electrical tape that might not have sent a chill through my body if it hadn't been sitting on top of a crumpled white sheet of canvas.

But it couldn't be the same one I saw in the forest behind the factory that night, the one sheltering the trove of artwork.

The artwork that Aaron apparently drew . . .

Anyway, the real prize is the TV. It's big and clunky with a small, bulbous screen that's fractured in so many places, it might as well not be there at all. The device looks like it's been broken off its wall mount. I instantly think of the security camera that had at one point guarded the perimeter of the factory while EarthPro vied for the land. This was likely a security monitor.

I decide this is worth a pause in my fight with Enzo. There'll be time for all kinds of arguing after this. Right now, I've just stumbled upon our very first engineering project.

I stand and start to make my way back into the hallway, when I pass a grimy window that looks out on the front of the factory. I can see the head of the path leading to the park.

Just as I'm about to turn around, I see Enzo.

After propping his push broom against the nearest tree, he starts to head down the path, then stops and stands in place for a minute. He turns and looks at the factory, and I think he's going to come back. He's going to change his mind and stay here working this lame job with me. He's going to set our fight aside, too, and remember that we're the same kids who play video games together and attend boring pep rallies and eat sushi and share a geekiness that would lead us to form a club named after a giant flightless bird.

He's going to remember that we're friends.

Instead, he turns around and gives the entrance of the factory a final look, then walks away.

I've felt alone many times in my life. It's just a product of moving. And being alone doesn't always mean I'm lonely. Sometimes it's nice to only have to worry about myself, to eat an entire block of cheddar cheese because I feel like it, to drag out my old collection of action figures and not have someone laugh at me.

But that's not the kind of alone I feel now. I feel the kind of alone that only appears when you realize you can't fill all the empty pieces of yourself. At some point, other people need to give you some of those missing pieces, too.

I make my way down the stairs I don't even remember climbing to get here. I set my broom in the middle of the floor and close the factory door behind me, not that it matters if it's open or closed. I remember the broken TV and consider going back, but I'm not excited about it anymore.

Instead of walking down the path toward the park, I decide to walk the long way around the factory. I don't want to risk running into Enzo.

At the back of the factory, I look out of habit or some unconscious impulse toward the tree where the makeshift art studio used to be, its contents protected from the elements by a canvas tarp. I might have been so close to finding Aaron and Mya that night, and I didn't even know it. If only I'd looked for clues in those drawings a little bit harder. There have been so many times that they've felt just out of my grasp, like they were on the other side of a thin veil, and if only I paid close attention, I'd be able to see them.

Today, though, instead of finding a tree trunk with a shredded piece of rope tied to the bark, I see a fluttering piece of paper, waving me toward it on the end of a light breeze.

"What?"

I unfold the paper, and it's a pencil drawing of a face, one not unlike that drawn onto the head of the mannequin in Mrs. Tillman's store. But while that face was crude, this drawing's face is distorted. Its eyes are wide, its cheeks deeply sunken. Its nose is long and points to a mouth parted only enough to show its bared teeth.

The rest of the page is shaded, making the head look as though it's poking out into the light for the first time in ages. I want to fold the paper up and put it right back where I found it, but I can't bring myself to stop looking at it. Maybe because its eyes seem to pull me in.

Or maybe because as grotesque as this drawing of a face is, there's no mistaking that this face is Aaron's.

I finally bring myself to fold it up, when I realize there's something written on the back of the paper. When I turn it over, I see a more familiar picture—that of Aaron and Mya, all smiles in their snapshots, their descriptions listed under the word "Missing."

Chapter 7

I t's the first semi-cool day we've had all summer, and the timing couldn't be better, because every single person in Raven Brooks is going to be outside.

It's groundbreaking day.

"Did you fill the silver thermos with water?" Mom asks as she rummages through her purse, and Dad and I exchange an is-she-talking-to-you-or-me? look.

"Either one of you will do," she says, and Dad takes this one.

"Was just on my way," he says, and Mom utters something indecipherable.

"Nicky, you haven't told us much about that club you and your friends are starting. Are Trinity and Maritza planning to join, too?" Mom asks, and she's terrible at pretending to be casual. A scientist to the end, she's not super big into small talk; she prefers chatter that has a purpose. There's always an answer to be found.

"I have no idea," I say, and I'm not lying. At one point, EMU was all of us. Now I couldn't say who or what it is.

"Interesting thing about emus," my dad says from the

pantry. He's pretending to find the thermos, but I know I heard a wrapper opening in there. "They're a flightless bird, but they use their wings for cooling off. I guess they flap them around like a fan or something."

"Sweetie, is everything okay with you and your friends? It seems like you've been spending more time at home than normal."

"So what, you think the problem is with me?" I ask defensively. I guess I'm not that good at faking it, either. I'm totally dreading seeing them today at the groundbreaking, but there's no getting out of it. We're "being a part of the community."

"They also use their wings to steer," Dad says from the pantry. "Like rudders!"

"I didn't say you were the problem. But statistically speaking, there's a 25 percent chance you are," she says.

"Well, there's a 100 percent chance that this conversation is lame," I say.

"They're also nomadic. They follow the food source. Not a lot of people know that," Dad says.

"Lame or not, you're hiding something," Mom says, and it's a little early in the morning to be feeling like a criminal.

"It's just . . . I'm just . . ."

I'm just tallying the cost of a bus ticket to an unpopulated desert.

I'm just peeling the paint from the corner of my room for hours at a time.

I'm just waiting for the Aliens to get it over with already.

"I'm just taking some time to think," I say, and Mom looks unconvinced, so I add, "About my future."

She seems to consider this for a second, and to break eye contact with her right now would be to expose my lie in all its naked, fibbing glory.

"Okay," she says. "Just know that there's an expiration on the quietly-thinking-alone-in-your-room thing. There's a fine line between being an intellectual and being a shut-in."

I nod, and Dad chimes in from the pantry.

"The fastest one has been clocked at just over thirty miles per hour! Can you believe that?"

"That's fascinating, Jay, and I'd like to know more about how you've acquired all of this emu knowledge, but right now, all I care about is the thermos, so can you please finish your Ding Dong so we can leave?"

* * *

We arrive at exactly the same time as Trinity and her parents, and it takes everything in me to act nonchalant as Trinity avoids eye contact with me.

"This spark of brilliance had to go through at least five different approvals, and yet it dawned on NO ONE that hosting a fair right next to the old fairgrounds that the town *burned down* might be a tad inappropriate," says Mom.

"Never proven," says Mr. Bales.

Trinity and her mother and my parents all stare at Mr. Bales.

"What? It could have been an electrical fire. It could have been badgers."

We blink.

"They're all over the woods! They can be very destructive. They chew through wires, don't they?"

Dad is about to short-circuit. So. Many. Jokes.

"Nicky, take me away. Quick, before I irreparably mortify your mom."

Dad and I volunteer to search for shaved ice and programs, in that order.

All around us, the townspeople of Raven Brooks pretend to have as much fun as we're pretending to have. The decision has long been made to develop the land. Even if we changed our minds, it's too late to turn back now. EarthPro has officially set up shop, with portable offices staged between the old park and the old factory, right here where they've decided to hold the groundbreaking ceremony. They've been rolling cement mixers and excavators down the centerline of town every day for the past week.

Big Business has come to Raven Brooks. It all seems to have happened overnight.

Still, not everyone is happy. There are the small business owners eyeing the promotional tents EarthPro has set up. Corporate people are giving away Frisbees and balloons and pens and pocket flashlights. I roll one of the flashlights from the table and slip it into my pocket. I may not be happy they're here, but there's never a bad time to carry a pocket flashlight.

Then there are the EarthPro people who are giving Mrs. Yi a wide berth. They're well aware that she's the reason they are here, but they're also aware of the tenuous line they have to walk between enthusiasm and greed. No one dares evoke the name Lucy Yi.

"You see Miguel anywhere?"

Then there's Dad. He and Enzo's dad have been doing their best to be objective, but their core differences never really faded. Just because they came to the same decision about what should be done with the land, that doesn't mean they arrived at it the same way.

"Nope," I say.

"I'm guessing you don't care, either?" he says, and it takes me a second to catch his hint.

"So you know?"

"Narf, you're about as stealthy as an elephant. You're not so great at hiding things."

I look down at the shaved ice I've been holding but not actually eating. It's starting to drip blue streams down my hand as it slowly melts.

"You boys have had your differences before, and you worked it out," Dad says, and part of me wonders if he's saying that for his own benefit, too. He's still looking around for Mr. Esposito.

"You'll patch things up," he says.

"I'm not sure I want to," I say, and hearing it aloud makes it sound awfully final.

"Nah," Dad says dismissively. "That's your pride talking. Once teenage insecurity kills the last of your pride off for good, you'll forgive and forget."

"Thanks, Dad. That's not bleak at all."

"I bring you words of wisdom from my many years of dumb decisions," he says. Then he does finally look at me. He waits for me to look up from my dripping snow cone.

"The most interesting people are often misunderstood, Nicky," he says. "People usually think geniuses are loonies before they realize they're, well, geniuses."

How did he know what was wrong? I mean, "*genius*" is taking it a little far, but it seems like he's talking about me. But then I remember Dad always seems to know.

"I'm not sure," I say. "What if they're just . . . I dunno . . . a lost cause?"

Dad shakes his head slowly. "Nothing's ever really lost. Sometimes you just need to clear the debris to find it."

I think of all the debris in my pathetic life: swept into piles in the factory, hauled to an outbuilding in the park, thrown into the darkest corner of my closet. It's hard to believe I'll ever crawl my way to the surface.

"Attention! Attention, friends of this fine town!"

A man in a light-brown suit stands on the stage they've erected for the occasion. He's wearing the telltale EarthPro hard hat that looks as unnatural on his head as it did on Ms. Delphine's.

"Welcome! Thank you for joining us on this very special day. We are so pleased to see such a stellar turnout."

Low-level applause ripples through the crowd, spreading like a germ. It appears to have dawned on more people than just my mom that this event might be a tad insensitive given the locale's history. It's kind of obvious that we're all ready to just get this over with. A circle of friends buffers Brenda Yi by the side of the stage while the rest of the crowd pays more attention to her than to the EarthPro guy.

"There he is," Dad says, and I see Mr. Esposito, weaving through the crowd as he makes his way toward us, his hand extended to my dad before he even gets close. They fall into an easy hug/back slap and start cracking jokes right away. My stomach twists in a little knot of jealousy over their friendship.

To my surprise, Enzo follows behind him and immediately pulls me aside.

"I need to talk to you," he says, leaning close to my ear.

"Really? Might be dangerous standing next to me. I am a maniac, you know," I say, not bothering to look at him. Suddenly, I'm very interested in what the EarthPro dude is saying. Evidently, the homes they plan to build will be equipped with the latest in residential technology.

"I'm serious," he says. "It's important, and I want you to hear it from—"

The crowd applauds loudly this time, and at first, I think it's about the solar panels they intend to install on the roofs, but then I see that the EarthPro dude has stepped to the side of the microphone and invited Mrs. Yi to say a few words, which is either the best idea or the world's worst call. Either way, we all stand at attention, eyes forward, mouths closed. All of us except for Enzo.

"Nicky, listen to me."

"Shhhhh," the woman in front of us admonishes, giving Enzo a solid once-over before turning back around. Mr. Esposito leans backward to give Enzo a warning look, and he shuts up, but he's still squirming all over the place.

"Friends, it's good to see you all here, celebrating what I believe is the new beginning to a very bright future for Raven Brooks," Mrs. Yi says, her calm voice in no way relinquishing its strength. She's impossible not to listen to.

But Enzo isn't giving up. He nudges me, and I turn to face him for the first time. He looks awful, like he's coming down with something. His hair is sticking up in strange places, and I think maybe he hasn't showered, either. My face flushes hot as I realize this is probably how I look half the time these days.

Still, I shrug him off.

"Your continued support has not only meant the world to me, but to *us*," Mrs. Yi says. "It's critical that, as we celebrate this new beginning, we embrace it together, as a community."

The quietest of murmurs travels through the crowd as they decide Mrs. Yi is right.

I feel a tap on my shoulder, and I'm about to tell Enzo to bug off when I see Ms. Delphine standing there instead. Suddenly, I'm Mr. Popular.

"Nicholas, Enzo, so happy to see you two have already had a chance to talk," she says.

"No, no, I was just—" Enzo starts, but the woman in front of us turns around, and this time she means business. Her face is screwed up so tight, I think it might cave in.

Ms. Delphine draws back with her hands up. "Of course, so sorry." Then she motions me to a corner far away from the crowd.

Enzo grabs my arm to keep me from going, but unless he's planning to apologize for being such a royal jerk—and he hasn't done it yet—then I don't really care what it is he's dying to tell me.

I pull out of his grip and join Ms. Delphine in the corner by the shaved ice stand. She's wringing her hands, and I'm distracted by the glossy red nails she can't seem to stop fidgeting with.

"I do hope you understand. When I said yes, I had no idea that it was against the rules to say yes to both," she says, and I catch a glimpse of genuine remorse under the shade of her hard hat.

"Huh?"

"And given that it appears that your membership numbers have, er, shifted recently, and theirs have, well, grown . . . and theirs is really more in line with my work anyway . . ." she says, and now she's squirming like Enzo was, and seriously, *what is going on*?

"Sorry, you're going to have to back up," I say, scratching my neck. The beautiful day this started out to be has suddenly turned uncomfortably hot.

"Your little club," she says, and I can't tell if she meant for it to be condescending, or if that's just her. "Engineering . . . um Mutants of—?"

"*Masters* of the Universe," I say, and wow, kinda hard to be indignant when I say it aloud.

"Right. Well, given that you are now the sole member, and—"

"Wait, wait. Hold on a sec," I say, but my stomach drops to the dirt ground because it seems to catch on a split second before my brain does.

"Oh no. Oh gosh. I thought Enzo told you," she says, and now Ms. Delphine looks like she wants this to be over with more than I do.

"Enzo's quitting?"

"Evidently, there's a new club, and—"

The crowd applauds, and the man in the brown suit returns to the stage.

"Thank you, Brenda Yi, for your insightful words. And now I'd like to welcome to the podium Ms. Angelica Delphine, our executive vice president of Community Outreach for EarthPro. Angelica has a special certificate she'd like to present to some very enterprising youngsters here in the town of Raven Bridge."

An aide from the side of the stage hustles over to the man in the brown suit.

"Raven *Brooks*," he corrects, then clears his throat a little too loudly. "Angelica, come on up and say a few words."

The man onstage sounds desperate, and though Ms. Delphine hasn't finished explaining how she's ditched me in favor of sponsoring another club, she steps carefully through the crowd and eventually makes her way to the microphone, adjusting it to her height as feedback from the speakers fills the air.

"Thank you, Dave, and thanks to all of you for welcoming us into your hometown with loving arms," she says, and a low murmur moves through the crowd. Loving arms?

"As executive vice president of Community Outreach, one of my most important jobs is to make sure EarthPro is building the future of this community through partnership with the brilliant young minds of the future. After all, our children hold the key to the innovations of tomorrow."

I start to roll my eyes, but her mention of the word "key" only reminds me of the note left at the bottom of the trellis under my window: RED KEY.

Okay, it's official. I'm absolutely, 1,000 percent obsessed.

"To that end," Ms. Delphine continues, "I am proud to welcome to the stage an intrepid young woman, who has taken it upon herself to establish the first human rights organization at her school: Creating Responsibly Outsourced Work, or CROW as we've begun to call it. So, without further ado, I'd like to present this certificate of partnership to the club's founder, Trinity Bales. Trinity, come on up!"

I didn't think my stomach could sink any farther into the ground, but apparently there's all kinds of room for it to fall, and if only my stomach could take me with it. If only I could crawl into a hole and never ever come out.

Trinity is far away, practically on the other side of the crowd, but I see her anyway. I see her because she wants me to see her. She's staring hard at me, and the normally confident, dark eyes I used to take so much comfort in now look like they're brimming with tears.

Or maybe that's my own stupid eyes. Who could tell from this far away?

I hear Trinity thank Ms. Delphine. I hear her calm, passionate voice speaking softly but confidently into the microphone. But I don't hear a word that she says. I listen all the way to the end, but I can't hear a thing.

I see Enzo as I pass him, but I don't hear what he tries to tell me.

I see Mom chatting it up with the EarthPro people in charge of community funding, and she tries to wave me over, but I pretend not to see her.

I feel eyes on me, but I try not to turn around. It's only when Maritza stands directly in front of me that I have to stop.

"Nicky, we're sorry, okay?" she says, but she doesn't sound sorry at all.

The crowd is all mingling again, and the commotion should be enough to drown out the screaming I'm doing in my head, but nope. My internal raging voice is coming in crystal clear, and Maritza is precisely the last person I want to see right now.

"Sorry for what exactly?" I say. "For ditching EMU and taking Enzo with you? For stealing the only sponsor I could find? For icing me out basically the entire summer?"

"Nicky, she means it. We all mean it," Trinity says, making her way toward us. She and Enzo are standing behind me now.

"Yeah? Nice certificate," I say to Trinity with as much venom as I can drudge up, and she looks down, embarrassed, which makes Enzo step in.

"She *earned* that certificate."

I shift to Enzo. "EMU was supposed to be *your* club. Face it—the only reason you abandoned it was because you couldn't stand *me*."

"You kinda sucked all the fun out of it," Enzo says, and now he's looking at the ground with Trinity. I turn back around, and at least Maritza has the guts to look me in the eye while she betrays me.

"Oh, I see. So it's my fault."

We're starting to draw a crowd now, and I can't tell if my face feels hot because of embarrassment or anger or the sun that's suddenly scorching enough to melt us all into rivers of sweat.

"You were never interested in EMU in the first place!" Maritza blurts. "You just used it as an excuse to—"

"Guys, what's going on?" Mom says, looking equal parts mortified and worried. The EarthPro people behind her look concerned, and I know this would be the perfect time to stop my little tantrum, but it's all I can do to keep from throwing a snow cone in each of their faces right now.

"Enzo?" Mr. Esposito says from farther back in the crowd. "Everything okay?"

"Fine, Dad," Enzo says, still looking at the ground.

"Oh yeah. Better than fine. *Fantastic*," I say, my voice oozing with sarcasm.

"Nicky, tone!" Dad admonishes, and I know it must be bad when *Dad's* the one calling out my behavior.

I look straight at Enzo. "Sorry, Dad. It's just that I'm a little busy sucking all the fun out of things," I say, gritting my teeth. "It's what I'm best at."

"Nicky—"

"That's me, the fun devourer!" I wave my hands around wildly enough for people to have to step back. If we didn't have a full audience before, we have one now.

"I gobble up fun and spit it out. Tasty, tasty fun! Nom nom nom!"

I feel hands press into my shoulders and hear Mom's voice in my ear whispering something about calming down, and I can see Dad moving quickly through the crowd, but I can't seem to stop myself. The entire town of Raven Brooks is playing spectator to my unhinging, and I'm so angry—so ridiculously over-the-top delirious with rage—that all I can do is insist on giving them the show they've all been waiting for.

"Or maybe, just maybe, you quit EMU because despite everything you've seen—that WE'VE ALL SEEN"—I flail, casting my ire onto Trinity and Maritza, too—"you think I'm the one who's CRAZY! That's what you all want me to be, right? Crazy new kid Nicky here!"

It's like I'm speaking in tongues now. My dad is hustling toward me like he's trying to put out a fire, and Mom's pinching my shoulders so hard, I can hear a ringing in my ears, but I'm not finished yet. I haven't completely burned this ceremony down, and if there's one thing this park knows, it's how to catch fire.

"You're all so happy to finally hear me say it. That I'm as out of my mind as my bubbe! Now you can all go home feeling so much better."

"What's a bubbe?" I hear someone say.

"Maybe a donut or something?" someone else guesses.

"Or maybe I'm off my rocker like Mr. Peterson!" I rant.

Gasps all around.

"That's right. Now don't you feel so much better having someone to blame for all the messed-up things that happen in this messed-up town?"

"Nicky, stop!"

That was my mom. Hers was the last voice I heard before the white-hot anger consumed me completely.

Next thing I know, I'm running through the forest. I don't remember how I made it this far into the woods with no one following me. Maybe I managed to outrun my parents. Maybe nobody bothered to come after me. Maybe they were all so relieved that I left, I could have strolled away whistling, and they would have been fine with it. Whatever the case, I'm now in the wild in-between of the temporary EarthPro headquarters and the old park.

Just before the turn in the path, I look for the usual sign that I'm nearing the ruins of the park: The burned-out entrance should be visible just over the tree line. When I don't see it, I round the corner a little faster. Nothing could have prepared me for what I see next.

The park is just . . . gone. Every last piece of wood or metal or cement. Every last scorched remnant of the place the Golden Apple Corporation built atop the dreams of a small town, the place Mr. Peterson's deranged mind brought to life, the place where Lucy Yi smiled her last smile. Every last scrap has been razed in the name of forgetting.

And with it, any clue it might have held about Aaron and Mya has been erased forever.

I stare at the vast expanse of level dirt and wait for something to happen.

"This can't be it," I say, and I don't think I've ever felt more hopeless, more desperate for a way forward, than I do right now.

Just when my eyes begin to burn from staring for so

long, a wind kicks up out of the clear summer air. Way in the distance, in the far back of the park where the Rotten Core used to loom, I hear the dust devils before I see them. The sky has turned a dusky purple, and the groundbreaking will end soon. But I want to see this. I need to see this.

They twirl on their tiny tails, these swirls of dirt that seem to come from nothing, unwieldy on their small, inverted shapes, and the image of top-heavy robots balancing on tiny wheels skitters through my mind. I watch the dust devils rotate until they lull me into a daydream, and Bubbe Fein's words swirl through my head.

New dirt lets the fingers dig and pull. New dirt leaves spaces in between the granules. But old dirt . . . old dirt keeps its secrets held tight.

When the dust hurts my eyes too much, I finally decide to walk home, but the words my grandma used to say bother me the entire way.

"It has to mean something," I say into the wind, which has now kicked up considerably. People have been saying for days that a big storm is coming. This must be the start of it.

"All of this has to mean something."

Just then, from the opening in the trees ahead, a sheet of paper comes wafting toward me, nearly slapping me in the face as it passes. I reach out just in time to catch the corner of the page and turn it over to find Aaron and Mya staring back at me.

"You again," I say to the Missing poster, remembering a time I said that to Aaron through the window of my bedroom.

I reluctantly turn the poster over, bracing myself for another disturbing drawing, but this time I find a different depiction, though it's familiar, too. It's the exaggerated slope of a death-defying roller coaster, with a landscape of tiny terrified people looking on from below.

I walk a little faster through the break in the trees, making my way to Friendly Court to find it unnervingly quiet.

With everyone still at the groundbreaking, it's just me and the neighborhood cat.

Except I know that's not really true, because it's not completely quiet. The faint sound of carnival music wafts from somewhere in the Peterson house. I probably wouldn't even be able to hear it over the starting of a car or the rumble of a lawn mower.

Two more sheets of paper swirl in the now steady wind, and I snatch them from the air. Still more Missing posters, and two new sketches on the backs of these papers—one of a ballerina with hands in an arc over her head, her toes pointed, her tutu a halo around her waist. The other is simpler than the rest—a nondescript key.

"Red key," I mutter just before a handful of Missing posters float in my direction. I look up this time to see where exactly it is they're coming from and find the window to Aaron's bedroom wide open, his curtain waving as though reaching for the freed posters.

It would be the worst decision in the world to climb the tree outside of Aaron's window. This is exactly what every horror movie in the history of horror movies has tried to warn people *not* to do. Unsuspecting innocents are forever following some creepy sound or investigating that weird shadow. I've seen enough *Tooth* movies to know how this ends.

And yet, there are my feet on the gnarled sides of the trunk. There are my hands grasping for the lowest branch, then the one above that.

"I am dumber than the first victim in every single slasher flick," I tell myself. But I keep climbing.

When I'm at eye level with the window, I peer through the opening to find an empty room. Only now do I realize I was expecting beyond all reason to find Aaron sitting there at his desk, looking at me like he's been waiting for me to figure out the mystery forever.

The room isn't exactly as I remember it, though. It seems to have undergone a little renovation. Covering every inch of the wall are drawings on the backs of all the stolen Missing posters in Raven Brooks. Faces twisted in agony, ballerinas in perpetual point, rides of impossible proportions, keys without locks: Each drawing is shaded in pencil lead, the lines drawn quickly, almost frantically, in quick wisps that fade at the tips. I ease from the branch and pull myself into the room without giving too much more thought to the stupidity of being here because I can't quite understand what it is I'm seeing.

Another poster dislodges itself from the wall and floats out the window on a fresh wind while the rest of the papers grow restless as they await their turn to be free.

Everywhere I look, it seems that there are eyes looking at me—pleading with me—from the pictures on the wall.

And the closer I look, the more I realize that I have seen some of these before.

"Under the tarp," I breathe, recognizing a few of the more intricate scenes from that night behind the factory. Whoever took those pictures down didn't destroy the little makeshift studio; they just moved it.

I follow the art all the way to Aaron's desk, around the back wall and to his bunk bed, where I stop cold, my heart forgetting how to beat.

There in the bottom bunk, under the plaid comforter I slept with an eternity ago in that very bed, is the form of a body.

"It's not . . . it can't be. It's definitely not . . ." But I can't bring myself to say the words.

It can't be Aaron under there.

All it would take is two steps and one flick of the wrist to find out for sure. Just two steps, one quick pull, then it would be over. I would know. I would finally know.

I take the first step toward the bed and begin to shake violently. If I'd eaten anything more than a snow cone today, I might throw up.

I take the second step and swallow the hard knot in my throat that's keeping me from breathing.

I extend my hand and prepare to pull the comforter away, then retract.

It isn't him. It isn't him.

I reach again, then yank my hand away.

Please don't be him.

I reach for the third time, and this time I grasp the blanket so tight, there's no way I can let it go.

"One, two . . ."

I pull as hard as I can and squeeze my eyes shut. When I open them slowly, I find not the body of a boy, but the body of a mannequin, an electrical tape X over its mouth, a tiny piece of yellow crime scene tape still attached to its cylindrical torso.

"What?"

The dummy from Mrs. Tillman's store. But how did it get here, and why is it in Aaron's room under the covers, and what sort of sick game is this anyway?

I'm so shocked to see the mannequin here in Aaron's room that I nearly miss the jewelry box perched on its chest, right above where a beating heart might be.

I pick up the box carefully, lifting the top to reveal a tiny ballerina. She spins slowly on her pedestal in front of the mirror, a delicate song chiming from the inner workings of the box.

I search the jewelry box, pulling out little drawers and trays but finding nothing. I feel around the bed and look under the mattress. I slide my hands behind the mannequin and avoid looking at the drawn-on eyes. There has to be something here—something Aaron wanted me to find.

This was Mya's jewelry box. Maybe it wasn't Aaron who left it there. Maybe it was Mya. Maybe the answers aren't here at all, but in Mya's room.

But it isn't Aaron or Mya standing there when I turn around.

Mr. Peterson is wearing his argyle sweater. It's the middle of summer, and he has to be burning up, but his face betrays exactly nothing. His waxed mustache curls high on his lip, pointing to the eyes that are staring at me so intently, I wonder if it's possible to kill someone just by looking at them.

The wind from outside fills the room, lifting every single paper from the wall and creating a symphony of flapping.

Not an ounce of breath fills my lungs as I wait to see what he'll do. He's no more than a foot inside Aaron's room, but his presence takes up all the space we share. With one swipe of his arm, one stomp of his boot covered in black goo, he could wipe me out. A flick of his mustache, and he could vaporize me.

Yet he hasn't made a single move. He hasn't said a word.

I match his stare not out of bravery. I simply can't make myself look away. The window is miles from my reach, the tree outside a light-year away. Whatever Mr. Peterson decides is my fate, he will win. For the first time, I have no place to hide, nowhere to run.

I don't know how long we stand there, daring the other to move, refusing to be the first one. I hear the buzz of the streetlight as it flickers on. Mr. Peterson still hasn't moved.

Then, as the shadows from the street begin to pour through the room, his face does finally shift. Tiny crinkles form around the outer corners of his eyes, and there, underneath his waxed mustache, his teeth form the most horrific smile I've ever seen.

Then he begins to laugh.

Not a chuckle or a belly laugh. Nothing close to joy.

His voice is a high whine, like he's letting it out little bits at a time like air from a balloon. But if the laugh is coming from his mouth, I can't see how. It's almost as though it's coming from a hole deep inside of him.

The sound of his glee at my terror peels back the last of my nerves, and my legs threaten to give out.

Then, floating through the window on one of the stormy winds, the sound of my father's voice reaches us, answered by my mom's. I can't hear what they say, but that doesn't really matter. What I do hear are car doors slamming and front doors opening. The groundbreaking ceremony has ended, and the neighborhood has come back to life.

The laughing stops, but Mr. Peterson's grotesque smile stays glued to his face.

If I'm going to be allowed to leave this room, the moment is now. While the voices are still near and help is within screaming distance. Now is when I have to make my move.

I take the first step toward the window, and I watch Mr. Peterson carefully for the tiniest flex of a muscle. All that moves is his head, though, as he follows my motion toward the window, that horrifying grin promising to haunt me forever.

I set the jewelry box down on the bed and take another step. Again, he does nothing to stop me.

I take the last two steps fast, launching myself out the window carelessly, with complete disregard for my bones or anything else I might break on the way down. It would have taken one lunge—just one—for him to stop me, and I couldn't risk it.

But he didn't stop me.

Miraculously, I land on the branch that's level to the window and turn back around to make sure he hasn't tried to follow me out, or maybe run for the stairs and out the front door to wait for me at the bottom.

His wide, unblinking eyes watch me, but he hasn't moved.

My parents have gone inside, and the neighborhood is once again quiet. It's me and it's Mr. Peterson, staring at each other, separated by six feet and an open window.

I watch him until I can't see him anymore, until the window is above my head and I only have eyes for the ground and the street and then my yard and my front door, and the safety of being in the house with my parents, even if I don't want to talk to them or anyone else.

I run straight up the stairs to my room and lock the door behind me, then drop to the floor and hunker behind the window ledge below my own bedroom window. I risk a quick look across the street, but Aaron's bedroom window is closed. If Mr. Peterson is still in there, I wouldn't know it.

If he's watching me watch him right now, I would have no idea.

And just as promised, I fall into the worst sleep of my life that night, tossing and turning away from the betrayal of my friends, the disappointment of my parents, the mortification of my own actions.

Mostly though, I try and fail to hide from the image burned into my brain: the wide, smiling mouth of Mr. Peterson, the sound of that joyless laugh seeping through his pores.

Chapter 8

'm ripped from sleep the next morning by the angry growl of machinery.

The sun is again blindingly bright, but instead of welcoming me to the day, it assaults me like the sound outside. I stumble from bed asking myself why my dad would be mowing the lawn again so soon, but before I even set eyes on my window, I know that this sound is different.

This is the sound of a beast chewing.

I part the curtain to find Mr. Peterson massacring the massive oak in front of Aaron's window.

"No," I whisper, and I don't know if I'm mourning more for the blatant act of butchery or for the loss of such an ancient figure that really didn't deserve to go down this way, but it seems I'm not the only one gawking at the spectacle of it. Nearly every house on Friendly Court has a person on its driveway, slippered and robed, hair wrapped in curlers. I haven't seen this many neighbors on this street . . . ever. Not even at the town gatherings that I thought included the entirety of Raven Brooks. In fact, I'm not sure I fully believed each of these houses were actually occupied. But they're out now, all wondering what that tree did to suffer such an unceremonious death.

But I'm not. I know exactly why he's doing it.

Mr. Peterson takes periodic breaks, attacking the tree at different angles so as not to tilt it too far in the direction of the house. He's already stripped it of its many limbs, an act I can't believe I managed to sleep through. He's doing the job of at least three lumberjacks, and the sweat I can see pouring off his head proves it, sweat that I can't help but observe is likely only made worse by his insistence on wearing that Same. Argyle. Sweater. The only difference in his appearance from every other time I've seen him is his decision to wear protective goggles over his wide, unfocused eyes.

"Safety first," I say, but the joke falls flat even when there's no one to hear it.

Though eerily, it's almost as though Mr. Peterson *did* hear it, because no sooner do those two words leave my mouth, then he looks straight up at my window, keeping the jagged edges of the blade rotating along their column as he wipes the sweat from his brow and takes special care to make sure I know exactly why he's cutting down this tree.

If I thought I had an inroad to the Peterson house via Aaron's window, I was wrong. I might have been allowed to leave yesterday unscathed, but I'll never enter that house again.

If any of the dozen or so neighbors notice Mr. Peterson noticing me, they certainly don't seem too disturbed by it. Messy-haired heads shake and newspapers tuck under arms as people slowly drift back inside, talking into their coffee cups and stealing one last look over their shoulder at their eccentric neighbor across from the turquoise house.

I drag myself down the stairs and flinch at the clatter of pots and pans. In maybe the weirdest turn of events all summer long, Mom is standing over the stove, wielding a spatula like a weapon, while Dad labors over a proof of tomorrow's newspaper.

I stand in the doorway of the kitchen while I try to piece together an already bizarre morning.

"This is it," I say, and my dad peers over the rim of his reading glasses at me. "They finally did it."

"Who finally did what?" Dad asks, though he's only half-interested.

"The Aliens took me away. They dumped me in some backward universe where neighbors leave their houses and Mom cooks."

"Oh, a comedian! Just like your dad!" Mom says, and even though she doesn't turn around, I can feel her scowl.

Dad shoots me a warning with his eyes and nods in that way that tells me he needs me to cooperate right now.

"Narf, your mom is in charge of breakfast today because I have a deadline to meet," Dad says with unnerving normalcy.

I rummage through my memory of yesterday. I suppose it's possible that the whole scene I made at the ground-breaking, the embarrassment I caused with my meltdown, was an elaborate dream. I certainly enjoy my fair share of those. But it sure did feel real.

"Yesterday happened, right?" I ask, keeping it vague just in case I'm lucky enough to only have imagined it.

"Oh, it happened," Dad says. "It happened big."

"Jay," Mom warns, and it's clear they've rehearsed this conversation once or twice, and Dad isn't following the script.

"We think we owe you an apology," Mom says, glancing over her shoulder long enough for me to see that she means it. Her face is sweaty with the heat from the stove, but she looks miserable. She looks like she hasn't slept all night.

Then she sets the spatula down and faces me.

"We've been pushing you," Mom says, and oh holy Aliens she gets it. She actually gets it.

"It's possible—remotely possible," Dad says, "that we were a tad too wrapped up in our own worlds to understand how seriously this whole situation with your friends and the events of winter might be affecting you."

"And I think it was a good start to have you see Dr. Eisenkraft," says Mom.

So *that's* his name.

"But it would be foolish to think that it was a cure-all," Dad finishes. It's like they each agreed to take half of a sentence.

"Does that mean I don't have to see Dr. Eisenkraft anymore?" I ask.

"Nope. You're now going to see the Fern once a week," Dad says, and he winks at me.

"But yesterday wasn't entirely your fault," Mom says, turning to tackle breakfast again.

"Exactly. It was *spectacular*," Dad says, and Mom clears her throat loudly. "But it wasn't all on you," he finishes, and I suppose that's the best I can hope for after making such a spectacle of myself and ensuring that I burned every bridge that might lead me to a normal life in Raven Brooks, if "normal" was ever possible to begin with.

"And what your friends did to you was wrong," Mom calls over her shoulder, almost as an afterthought.

It's the first time this summer—maybe longer—that the knot in my stomach eases enough to let me smile. *Really* smile.

Because my parents may not believe anything I say about Mr. Peterson or Aaron or Mya or the broken tapes stashed in my closet or the Missing posters I didn't tear down or the mysterious "red key" message that was left for me.

But at least they're on my side. About this, they're on my side.

"Your mom is making *waffles*, Narf."

He says "waffles" like they're a new thing, and I nod along with him even though Mom isn't looking.

"Jay, you don't do condescension well. Where's the paprika?"

Dad looks like he's about to apologize when worry suddenly overtakes him. "Paprika in waffles. That sounds so . . ."

"Good?" I try.

"Try again," Mom scolds.

"Delicious," I say, no more convincing, but she seems satisfied.

"I'm just following the recipe," she says in answer to my dad.

"Um . . . which cookbook are you using, darling?"

"Ugh," Mom says, shaking something from her hand that looks weirdly viscous. "Now's not the time to start experimenting with nauseating new nicknames."

Dad gives up and goes back to his paper.

"Nicky, can you grab me the breadcrumbs?"

I don't bother to argue with Mom. Besides, I'm too distracted to think about paprika-and-breadcrumb waffles. The chain saw is buzzing away outside, and I'm still not fully convinced I didn't wake up in an inside-out universe.

I hand Mom the breadcrumbs as Dad flashes me a thumbs-up and goes to take a swig of his coffee before realizing his mug is empty.

"I'll get you more," I say, and Dad hands me his cup with a sigh.

"Bless you, child," he says, and trains his focus back on my mom, who is standing over something that's boiling hard enough to leave little spatters all over the stovetop.

"I don't understand why it's doing this," Mom says. "It's just supposed to be simmering."

"Is it?" Dad asks, and it's a fair question because I've never made waffles, but I don't think they simmer.

I set Dad's coffee down and start to make my way upstairs before he stops me.

"Hold up there, Narf. It's almost breakfast time," he says with the panicked look of a baby antelope that's about to be abandoned in a lion's den.

"Um, I'm not really . . ."

But Dad has another look in his repertoire. And I think this look is saying something to the effect of *If you ever hope to enjoy another Ho Ho in your lifetime, you will sit here and eat this unholy creation that your mom is cooking for us.*

I slowly make my way back to my chair like I'm marching to my death and sink into the seat while Mom curses at the pot she's stooped over.

"Maybe he needs the wood to build a time machine or something," my dad says, picking up what I guess was a conversation from earlier.

"I heard he was in a plane crash on a desert island way back in the seventies," Mom says, calling it quits at the stove.

Dad and I both look at her.

"What? You're not the only two who enjoy a little gossip once in a while," she says defensively.

Mom serves the "waffles" in bowls.

"Oh!" Dad says like it's a surprise that we're *not* getting waffles.

"I think they came out a little soft," Mom says, and this might be the only time I've seen Mom look less than confident. It's remarkable, too, because she can unwind the molecular makeup of penicillin, but a step-by-step recipe in a book seems to be weirdly out of her grasp.

"I think it'll be delicious," Dad says, and maybe this is what love is. All the tension in Mom's shoulders seems to slide away as soon as Dad grabs some spoons from the drawer and kisses Mom on top of her head. Because even this man who loves nothing more than dessert for breakfast can't hold it against my mom that she took that away from him. He must love her more than he loves maple syrup.

By the time we're done slurping our breakfast from spoons and I've gotten mostly accustomed to the flavor of paprika over uncooked waffle batter, Mom and Dad are laughing again, and I've managed to block the sound of the wood chipper for long enough to remember what it was like before the Petersons occupied all my time.

"How much longer is that racket going to go on?" Mom says, wincing at the commotion across the street.

"He even rented a stump grinder and a wood chipper," Dad says, setting his red pencil down and giving up on his proof. "I saw him parking it behind his house."

"What?" I ask.

"The backyard," he says, lifting his eyebrow at me.

"By the basement doors?" I ask, failing miserably at sounding casual.

"Um, yeah, I guess so. There's a fence—well, there used to be a fence—but he pulled out a few of the boards for some reason. Maybe to plug the thing in, I don't know," Dad says, and his finger pushes against his temple like it's all a little too much for him this early in the morning.

The phone rings just as we're clearing away the dishes.

"Channel Four is sending a news crew to the dig site," Dad says to Mom, hanging up the phone.

"Are you kidding me?" Mom says. "How much video do they need of machines digging in the dirt?"

"I don't know, but if Channel Four is there . . ."

"I know, I know. So are you," Mom says, waving Dad away as he pours the rest of his coffee into a travel mug.

How much video do they need of machines digging in the dirt?

Video.

Digging.

Dirt.

"Thanks again for breakfast, Mom," I say as I practically knock my chair over standing up.

"You're welcome, Ni—"

I'm already upstairs in my room, taking my place at the window again. Mr. Peterson has finished the sawing and is fully in the wood-chipping stage, but that's not what I'm looking at, either. I'm looking at the missing boards behind the wood chipper, the spot in the side yard where the extension cord runs to an outlet I can't see. What I can see in the backyard, though, is a hole in the ground where some loose dirt should be. Instead, the loose dirt is piled beside the hole, a shovel discarded nearby, an empty grave where a canvas bag once lay.

"He knows."

I dive into my closet and toss aside the boxes of extra parts and dismantled machinery, and on my life I swear I'm surprised to find a laundry hamper in there, too.

"Where did you come from?"

But there's no time to worry about laundry now. I grasp the dirt-crusted handle of the bag filled with VHS pieces and slide it from its hiding spot. Unzipping the bag and examining the contents gingerly, I feel as though I'm opening some sort of sarcophagus.

I zip the bag back up and rummage through the boxes of spare parts to find what I'm looking for: a roll of scotch tape, a screwdriver, the pen flashlight I snagged from groundbreaking day, my lockpick set, scissors, an old radio speaker, a magnifying glass, and two AV cables.

"Think, Nicky, think," I say, pushing my palm to my forehead as I try to envision the trove of security equipment I found at the factory the day Enzo and I had our big fight. There were cords, the electrical tape, the busted TV.

If I could figure out how to repair the TV, maybe—*maybe*—I could play the tapes.

"*If* you could even put the tapes back together," I say, already talking myself out of it. "*If* you could figure out how to play them back without a VCR."

I could just try to put the tapes together here, then sneak downstairs and use our VCR.

Except that half of what I need is at the factory. And besides, that's hours of work I'll have to spend looking over my shoulder, worried that Mom or Dad might be checking in on me. Clearly, I'm in need of checking on these days. What if they caught me using the VCR?

Gee, Narf, whatcha doing downstairs in the middle of the night watching creepy home videos of the neighbors?

That'll earn me at least two more sessions a week with Dr. Fern.

Nope. In this new inside-out universe, borrowing my parents' VCR and hauling it to an abandoned candy factory is the most logical decision.

"This is nuts this is nuts this is nuts," I tell myself, but it's for Aaron and Mya, and that makes it okay. Even if it's completely not okay.

As quietly as I can, I sling the canvas bag over my shoulder, then crack my bedroom door open and peek into the hallway to listen for my mom. Instead, I see her sitting on her bed, a stack of student lab reports fanned out before her, a red pen gripped firmly in her hand.

With Dad at work and Mom busy grading, there's a chance I could slip downstairs into the living room undetected.

I throw on some clothes, return the contents of my closet to their previous state, and edge into the hallway.

Then I wait. It feels like forever, but I seize my chance when Mom's pen rolls off the side of the bed and she ducks to retrieve it.

I dart down the hallway, taking care to jump over the two floorboards in the middle that creak. Halfway down the stairs, I hear her.

"Nicky?" she calls, and I hold my breath and wait for her to call to me again. When she doesn't, I wait another second before I hear her sigh, and the rattle of disappointing lab reports resumes.

At the bottom of the stairs, I make a slight detour into the pantry, grab three granola bars, and creep into the living room.

"Steady," I tell myself as I slide the VCR from its cubby in the television stand, the cords dragging along like tails and resisting when I pull.

Twisting my arm, I manage to yank the cords from their sockets, and maybe it's fear of getting caught that keeps me from thinking too hard about how or where I'd plug this thing in once I get to the factory.

Details, I tell myself. *Problems for later*. I'm in full obsession mode now. Mr. Peterson has thrown the gauntlet by blocking my path to the house. There's zero doubt in my mind that I've gotten close. I've come within striking distance of an answer he doesn't want me to find, and I have precious little time to discover what secrets these videos are hiding.

I wrap the cords around the VCR and shoulder the canvas bag before deciding that the back door would be safest. I can't risk Mr. Peterson—or anyone for that matter—seeing me leave. I need time to work, which means I need to leave undetected.

I escape Friendly Court to the chorus of the wood chipper and an otherwise regular morning, but this morning is nothing like the others. This is the morning I'm going to discover, once and for all, what Mr. Peterson is so determined to keep buried.

I enter the path to the woods with more focus and determination than I think I've ever had. My parents would be so proud, if only I were putting my powers toward a healthier end.

"This will all be over soon," I tell myself, and for some reason, I actually believe that. Something feels different about this day. Something feels . . . *possible.*

I ride that wave of determination all the way to the old Golden Apple Amusement Park.

Soon, cement will cover this old ground, and houses will rise on top of the cement, and normal families will live normal lives above what used to be the symbol of what went so wrong in Raven Brooks. The tragedy will be erased for good, and with it, any collateral damage will disappear.

But I refuse to believe that Aaron and Mya are collateral damage.

My heart is at the back of my throat as I speed-walk as quietly as I can the rest of the way to the factory, feeling more criminal than ever, yet I've never felt more right.

When I reach the perimeter of the factory, it's time to leave the protection of the trees. But I'm on high alert for pursuing footfalls, which is probably why I hear the crunching of dried vegetation from somewhere behind me, tromping down the same path I traveled a second ago.

I dive for cover behind an even thicker bramble among the trees, scratching my palms and cheek while I duck for cover. I drag the canvas bag against my chest and hunch my back, guessing my head would be a bigger giveaway than a black shirt.

There's something very familiar about the steps I hear approaching. My stomach drops with a sort of muscle memory, and I begin to panic because I know I should recognize whoever is behind those footfalls, but my mind is scrambling, and my hands are sweating.

This can't be it. I can't stop now. Not when I'm this close.

Soon, the first set of footfalls is joined by what sounds like a second set.

Why is this sound so familiar?

Leaves crunch underfoot, and I can tell they're getting closer. I hear what sounds like heavy breathing.

I want to pick my head up and look for an escape route, but I'm terrified to move. The sound is nearly on top of me now.

This can't be the end.

But I think it is. I think it's really over this time.

I feel hot breath on the back of my neck, and my entire body seizes up.

I squeeze my eyes shut as the heat on my neck grows.

Then it sneezes.

I'm paralyzed for maybe a full minute before I realize that whoever just sneezed on me is now sniffing the waistband of my shorts, then nosing underneath me to try to get to the canvas bag.

I uncurl my body and slowly turn to find myself face-to-face with a llama. Actually, two llamas. One of them is just a tad braver than the other.

"Margaret! Margaret, what've you found over there? Get back here, feisty devil!"

I can't seem to look away from the giant brown eyes that're so close to mine, with fringy lashes blinking and nostrils blowing air hard enough in my face to ruffle my hair.

"See what a bad influence you are on Frederick? You know he does whatever you do."

Seconds later, actual human footsteps approach, and even if I could move—which I absolutely cannot—it would be pointless. I've been found out.

"Oh!" Farmer Llama seems just as surprised to see me as any normal person would be to find themselves in a staring contest with a llama.

"Margaret, give the boy some space, for heaven's sake. Whatever he has in there, he's not gonna give it to you if you go begging like that."

He turns to me.

"Ya got a granola bar on ya?"

I blink at him the way Margaret blinks at me. Somewhere inside of me, I muster the motor function to nod.

"Yeah, she loves granola bars," Farmer Llama says. "Beats the heck out of those health-nut Surviva bars. Give 'er wicked toots, if you catch my drift."

I have zero idea of what to say to this fact about Margaret.

"Well," Farmer Llama says, scratching the back of his head and looking at me like I'm the crazy one. "Get up if you want to. They don't attack. Well, not my kids anyway. Now Pat Meyer's beasts, that's another story, if you know what I mean."

Nope. Not a clue. But I nod because he's offered me his age-speckled hand, and I take his surprisingly firm grip to get back to my feet, keeping the canvas bag tucked behind my legs despite Margaret's insistence on getting a closer look.

Farmer Llama looks at the bag, too, then looks at me, worried, but maybe not worried enough to get into a whole conversation about it.

"I reckon I interrupted some important business out here," he says, not sounding sorry, but maybe . . . a little amused?

He gives the canvas bag behind my legs one more hard look before finding my eyes, and I hope he doesn't see the fear that lingers in them because I'm still not fully sure I'm out of danger.

"Come on, kids. Best grazing's up by the weather station," he says, looking at me one last time, but his llamas respond to his gravelly voice immediately. Frederick backs away first, followed by a reluctant Margaret.

Farmer Llama makes a gentle clicking sound, and they trot off ahead of him while he turns around, ambling away from me as though whatever just happened here was the most normal interaction one might have on a late Saturday morning.

I watch them walk halfway down the path toward the railroad tracks and the edge of town, before Farmer Llama turns back to me, his voice muffling what might be a laugh.

"You know, I woulda just given you the sign. All you had to do was ask," he says. And then he does laugh. He laughs hard enough to startle the llamas, but it doesn't seem to faze him.

Something tells me my face is sort of like those llamas right now: bewildered, mildly annoyed . . . but mostly shocked.

For the millionth time, I wish Aaron were here with me right now.

When Farmer Llama and his companions have rounded the corner, I do what I can to regain some semblance of composure and stoop to pick up the canvas bag before making my way to the front doors.

I'm disappointed, however, to find them locked.

"A scout is always prepared," I tell myself before reaching into the bag for my pick set. I brush aside the acknowledgment that I was never a scout, and besides, there's no merit badge for breaking and entering.

The lock is stubborn, but not as stubborn as I am. I just faced down two llamas and a wronged farmer. This lock can't get the best of me.

The factory is just as Enzo and I left it, complete with the push broom I abandoned on our ill-fated day of "work" with Ms. Delphine. I close the doors behind me and make my way up the stairs, carefully retracing my steps to the security room I stumbled upon the last time. To my relief, everything is still there.

"Here goes everything," I say, breathing a deep sigh before emptying the contents of the bag onto the floor and spreading out each piece of material. I take inventory of all the tools I have, put them aside, and begin the process of piecing the tapes back together.

To admit I'm flying blind would probably be enough to make me give up in the first five minutes, so instead, I try to pretend like it's a game. Luckily the room has a few blank tapes stashed away in a cupboard, so I start by pulling one apart to see how it works. With my screwdriver, I dispense five screws in the back and lift the flap up to reveal the rolls of

Mylar tape that hold the footage. I take careful note of how the mechanism inside looks and how the tape moves through each roller.

Then, using the EarthPro promotional pen light, I illuminate the former contents of the bag, pulling out the back of the first broken tape to get the clearest look at each torn edge. I know from the time our old VCR ruined Mom's copy of *The Wizard of Oz* that all the crumpled tape is useless—it can't be straightened out, and it won't play even if I rewind it onto the roll. As I cut away all the crumpled pieces, I wonder what memories, what evidence, are lost for good.

I roll my shoulders back from my neck and tell myself I'm not suppressing a chill; I'm just loosening my tense muscles.

When I've finally cut away all the bad pieces of tape, I line them up like tongues ready to talk, ready to be wound and placed in the open mouths of the new cassettes.

I line edge to edge until I think I might go blind from staring so hard at the delicate strands.

I eat my last granola bar.

I curse myself repeatedly for not bringing water.

I try to will feeling back into my numb shoulders.

I rub my eyes and wait for my vision to come back clearer.

And finally—*finally*—I have every piece lined up. I take each end and ever so carefully cut each torn edge at a slant, then join the two sides and adhere them with the Scotch tape. I think the work might never end, and I promise myself that this will be worth it. These excruciating efforts will be worth it.

I unwind a good chunk of the tape from the blank security cassettes and cut it away so there will be room for the repaired footage. Lifting the catch, I connect the found tape and rewind every reel. I place them on their fresh new spindles, nestling them back in their cases before closing the lid, reinserting the screws, and looking at what I've done.

I feel like Dr. Frankenstein.

"It's alive," I whisper.

After reassembling the tapes, I match each one up to the label that came off its original broken cassette. I come up with four tapes. The first tape had no label, but the others had dates.

12/29

4/5

8/22

The last of the day's sun glints off the lens of my magnifying glass. I've been here nearly all day, but I'm so close.

Then I look at my parents' VCR lying on the ground, waiting to be useful, and I slowly shake my head because I still have no idea how I'm going to power the machine to play the tapes.

"The generators!" I yell, startling myself.

I thunder down the factory stairs and run to the outbuilding, quickly examining each of the mini power sources before finding the one with an input that I think might just work with the AV cord.

I creep around the corner of the little shed on tiptoe like I'm in hot pursuit of a granola bar. Once I reach the doors, I finally catch a break. One door to the outbuilding is open.

I take one more quick look around and dart into the shed, immediately spotting a small generator against the back wall.

I peer over the top of the generator in search of the inputs, but it's too dark to see anything clearly, and I can't risk staying in here too long to research it. I'll just have to take my chances and move it.

Lifting the generator onto a nearby dolly proves to be harder than I thought it would, between its weight and awkward bulk, but I manage to walk it onto the edge of the cart and tip the dolly back. Now all I have to do is leave.

If I had a free hand, I'd brush the chill from my neck, but the weight of the generator is making my arms shake. So I think a quiet thank-you to the Aliens for giving me at least one small miracle today—a generator.

Back in the factory, I set the generator near the stairs and run an extension cord up to the security room. Then I connect the cord to the input, where it fits the plug perfectly.

My heart leaps, but there's still the problem of the shattered TV screen. No amount of tape or willpower could fix that problem.

"I need a screen," I say, realizing that the wall won't be light enough to project onto.

The white canvas is still crumpled where it was when I first found the room, and I shake it out and cough away the dust. There's a hole with a rivet on all four corners of the canvas, and I hang two of them on nails I hammer into the wall with the back of my screwdriver.

As I step away from the makeshift projection screen, I see a shadow of a familiar shape in one corner. With my penlight, I trace the lines of the sketch until the full picture comes into view.

It's the impossibly high arc of a roller coaster that should never exist.

It's only the hint of a picture, not even a full shape. More like the remnants of a drawing that started on paper and ran onto the canvas when the pencil met the paper's edge.

There's no denying that this is the canvas that covered the makeshift art studio behind the factory.

I back away from the screen and use my screwdriver to clear out the rest of the shattered glass from the screen. Inside the TV are three projection lights, the lights that usually project images onto the TV screen. Then I position the projection just right, tilting and focusing the rigged TV so that it shows the picture I brace myself to see.

Then I insert the first tape into the machine and press play.

The VCR hums loudly, and I think for a second I'm going to fry the tape inside it, but then I hear a series of clicks, and at last, the pieced together reel seems to catch hold of whatever it needs to catch inside the tape player, and a scene flickers to life on the canvas.

I have a chilling moment of déjà vu as I see Aaron's back, hunched over the desk in his room. The angle is slightly different, with the camera peering around the corner of his bedroom door, but the scratching of the pencil is all too familiar. It's just like my dream.

His room is not quite covered in drawings of the terrifying and exaggerated amusement park scenes like it was when I had my encounter with Mr. Peterson. Nor is it as crowded and frantic as the drawings that covered the make-shift art studio under the tarp behind the factory.

This is what I do to escape.

The camera shakes gently as a whisper of a giggle escapes from behind the lens.

"And now we see the Grumpy Older Brother species in his natural habitat."

Aaron turns toward the camera, and for the first time in almost a year, I see his face fully.

Not a nightmarish memory of him.

Not a Missing poster with a picture frozen in time.

It's actually Aaron. Looking annoyed and tired.

"Beat it, Pariah," he says.

"One must be careful to approach this breed with caution," she narrates.

Mya Pariah. I'm equally shaken by the sound of her long-missing voice.

Aaron turns back around, trying to slide a blank piece of paper over what it is he's drawing, but he's not quick enough.

The lens struggles for a minute to pull into focus the picture he's been drawing, but once it does, I hear Mya's breath catch just like mine does.

It's a picture of a tree as seen from its base, looking up. And there, obscured in the branches, is a lone roller coaster car.

"Is that supposed to be funny?" Mya says, her voice breaking.

The lens rests on Aaron's face, and I think I see regret before he says, "I'm not laughing, am I?"

I try to imagine Mya's expression, but I can barely decipher Aaron's, and I'm staring right at him.

There's another anguished moment of silence between them while they stare at each other, and then the picture cuts to static.

I steady my newly trembling hands and find the tape marked with the next date in sequence: 4/5.

The tape catches quicker this time, as though the VCR knows what to do with the mangled VHS, and sound filters through the old radio speaker first, quickly accompanied by an image of a different bedroom—Mya's. The camera shakes a tiny bit before it's motionless, and Mya appears before the lens, suddenly and ungracefully on her toes.

The music is immediately familiar, as is the source—it's the red jewelry box with the tiny ballerina in its center. The same red jewelry box that rested on the chest of the mannequin posed in Aaron's bed. Now it rests on a table under the bedroom window.

Mya dips and twirls unsteadily, and visions of that first home movie I didn't mean to see come back to me: the one of her mother reliving her dancing days before the weary eyes of Aaron and the wildly searching eyes of Mr. Peterson.

As Mya tries to emulate her mother in this new video, the tune from the jewelry box is slowly drowned out by the sound of arguing in the distance. I watch as Mya's distraction grows, her face tensing as she strains to hear what the voices are fighting about.

She lowers from her pointed twirl and moves behind the camera again, and the lens blurs from bedroom wallpaper to hallway wallpaper to the steps that make up the staircase leading down to the living room.

The camera roams until it finds its target, the tops of Mr. and Mrs. Peterson's heads, their hands gesturing with their hissed warnings and sudden outbursts.

"I'm not saying that. No one is saying that," Mrs. Peterson says, her hands pushing the air between her and Mr. Peterson, as though she's trying to calm a rabid animal.

"You don't have to say it, Diane. It's so obvious! Everyone knows what you think of me!"

"That's ludicrous!"

"So now I'm ludicrous?"

"Honey, no! You're putting words in my mouth."

"Why don't you just say it? Why don't you just come out and say what you want to say, Diane?"

"Okay, fine. You've changed. Ever since you moved your workshop down there, you've changed. You're . . . paranoid."

"Right. Of course. I'm paranoid."

Mr. Peterson starts to walk away. He looks like he's moving toward the kitchen, when he suddenly pivots and comes within inches of his wife. Even from this distance, Mrs. Peterson's effort to remain still is visible. She fixes her feet firmly to the ground, but every bit of the rest of her looks like it wants to flee.

"You have never understood me. *Never.*"

Mr. Peterson's tone is so menacing, I flinch from the canvas screen just as the camera jolts.

As though he hears me, Mr. Peterson whips around and glares directly into the camera. Mya and I gasp in unison, and I have to force myself to remember he can't actually see me.

But he could see Mya.

"What do you think you're doing?" he growls, and I can hear Mya's breath quicken behind the lens.

"I, uh . . ." I hear her say, but Mr. Peterson is already making his way toward the stairs.

"You think it's fun to spy on me, do you?" he says as he disappears from sight, presumably reaching the foot of the stairs.

"Ted, stop it. She didn't mean—"

"She didn't mean. *She didn't mean,*" Mr. Peterson's voice mocks, and the lens moves too quickly between the stairs and the living room and back to the stairs for me to see

Mrs. Peterson's expression. I just see her run for the stairs as Mr. Peterson growls:

"You're all against me. All of you!"

The camera drops to the ground and cuts out just as I think I'm going to pass out from holding my breath for too long again.

The VCR clicks, indicating it's reached the end of the tape, and I stare at it for a long time while I try to process what it is I just saw.

Staring at the floor, I notice I can barely see it anymore, it's gotten so dark.

Somehow, I managed to stay in the factory for the entire day, letting the evening slip into night without a second thought about how freaked out my parents might be.

I look back at the remaining two tapes and debate the risk of watching them.

But I'm already in enough trouble as it is. And if Mom and Dad have discovered the missing VCR . . .

"Oh boy."

I take the canvas down from the wall and cover my equipment, uneasy about leaving it. Then my criminal mind takes over, reasoning that if I leave the VCR here, I'll have a reason to come back.

Yes, Mom and Dad, I took the VCR—borrowed *it*—*and I'm ready for my punishment. But first, let me go back and get it.*

My sacrifice of freedom will be for a worthy cause.

I take one last look at the room and all it's shown me today before fleeing the factory and making my way back to Friendly Court, steeling myself for my parents' wrath.

Just as I round the corner, my toe catches a stray ball that's been abandoned in the middle of the street. Its hard, rainbow-striped shell actually hurts as I connect with it.

It's a moment that feels oddly familiar.

I watch the ball bounce and skitter down the street and roll to a stop right in between my house and the Petersons'.

With the tree cleared from the front of Aaron's house, it looks exposed. And I feel exposed standing in front of it, trying to kick the ball out of the street.

Glass shatters.

A scream comes from the Peterson house.

Mr. Peterson appears in the front window, fighting something.

Or someone.

As I creep closer to the front porch, trying to stay out of sight, I hear a gasp from Mr. Peterson. I'm right under the front window now, the one looking into the sitting room with the TV. There's another scream that goes suddenly quiet as Mr. Peterson slams the door to the basement.

A door that is now bolted with a bright red padlock the size of my hand.

A red padlock.

"Red key," I whisper.

Suddenly, there's a gasp from Mr. Peterson as he barrels toward me. I race away from the window and across the street, as fast as my tiny legs, atrophied from a summer sulking around my room, can carry me. The last things I see before throwing open the door to my house are Mr. Peterson's narrowed eyes, following me.

I'm not prepared to go from one chaotic scene to another. As soon as I'm through the threshold, my parents are practically on top of me, and I say the first thing I can think of.

"Oh, hey, guys."

"'Oh, hey, guys'?" my mom seethes. "'Oh, hey guys'?"

Dad squeezes her shoulder. "Lu."

"Do you have any idea how—?"

"Narf, we've been sick with—!"

"And you think you can just sneak—?"

"*Eleven* hours and—!"

"Not even a note to say—!"

"Did you take the VCR?"

They chew me out in unison; it's like they're performing the worst harmony ever.

I don't think they had any intention of stopping, except that when they manage to take a simultaneous breath, they step to the side, and to my surprise, Officer Keith is standing there looking like he's been practicing his "stern" expression.

"Mr. and Mrs. Roth?" he says after clearing his throat. "If you're ready?"

All three shift their attention back to me: Officer Keith looks puffed up on authority, Mom looks like she might tear my throat out with her teeth, and Dad looks embarrassed.

I follow them into the living room, dragging my stomach behind me because I'm pretty sure it dropped out of my body somewhere around the foyer.

They called the police?

I knew my parents were probably worried, but did they have to file a missing person report?

"Guys, I think maybe there's been a misunderstanding," I say, trying the practical approach, but my mom shoots me such a daggery look, I actually peek down at my shirt to check for wounds.

I follow them up the stairs, Officer Keith in the lead, as we head toward my room, and I have the most absurd thought that he's actually going to ground me while my parents look on.

"Seriously," I say, pushing my luck, but I can't help but feel like this is a huge overreaction, "I was just over at Enzo's and lost track of ti—"

Officer Keith pushes open my bedroom door, and I'm face-to-face with not only Enzo, but Trinity and Maritza, too. I'm not *eye-to-eye* with them, though. That would require them being able to look me in the eye, which they can't.

And it only takes me a second to see what they're staring at instead.

Scattered across the floor is a kaleidoscope of my crimes. There are the remnants of the radio I pulled apart to create the audio synthesizer for Mrs. Tillman's store. The wires I spliced for the dolls in Mrs. Bevel's shop. The springs I used for Mr. Quinn's mailbox. The St. Nick's Lovely Llamas sign.

But there's one part of this crime scene everyone seems to be focused on, and it's the one part I don't recognize, at least not as a part of my own mischief.

There, scattered among the loose lockpicks and radio parts, are dozens and dozens of Missing posters, faded and torn where the tape once stuck them to Raven Brooks' light posts and storefronts. Aaron and Mya, lost since last summer.

"Young man, did you tear these signs down?" Officer Keith asks, and how could he possibly think I did?

Except that everyone does.

Maritza stands with her arms crossed, glaring. Trinity looks embarrassed like my dad. Enzo can't stop shaking his head. Officer Keith looks awfully proud of himself. My mom . . .

My mom looks worried. She *never* looks worried.

"Of course I didn't!" I plead, but I might be a tad more believable if I hadn't been mid-lie when I opened the door of my bedroom.

"Nicky, I don't understand," Enzo says, and he really doesn't. I can tell. It's like whatever crumb of hope he'd been holding on to that I'm not totally out of my mind just got gobbled up by the Reality Monster.

"Are we seriously back to this? I've been the only one trying to *find* them!" I plead, but I have not a single supporter in this room to argue my case.

"See, now that's where we find ourselves in a pickle," Officer Keith says. "Because from my perspective, you seem to be the only one in possession of every bit of incriminating evidence," he says, and the energy in the room suddenly shifts.

My mom turns to my friends. "Enzo, you knew about this?"

"I didn't actually think—"

"Now hang on a second, Officer," Dad says, but it feels like maybe he's talking to everyone in the room. "You don't mean to imply that Nicky actually has something to do with these kids' disappearance."

"Of course he's not implying that," Mom says, shifting her posture to indignation, but her dismissal isn't taken lightly by Officer Keith.

"Actually, that's exactly what I'm implying," he says, and I don't even know if she does it consciously, but Mom pulls me in front of her, crossing her arms over my chest as though daring Officer Keith to take me from this room.

"I think that's an awfully big leap from finding some flyers to suggesting . . . I mean, you're suggesting . . ." Dad says, but he can't even finish it, and I'm so glad because to hear him say that I'm some sort of, what? Kidnapper? Or worse? I don't know if I could ever erase the sound of those words coming from his mouth.

"What I'm suggesting," Officer Keith says, threading his thumbs through his belt loops, "is that we have a longer conversation about this investigation down at the station. Say . . . tomorrow?"

Mom and Dad exchange a look I can't quite read. It's like they're trying to telepathically determine the right move here, and oh man, if they don't even know, then I really am in trouble.

I start to sweat uncontrollably. My neck is hot, and I can't feel my hands.

"So *now* there's an investigation?" Enzo says, and I can't believe I'm hearing it, but I couldn't be happier. "Because last I checked, there wasn't much interest in finding Aaron and Mya at all."

Enzo barely glances at me, but when he does, I swear I see a hint of hope. Like maybe he hasn't lost faith in me after all. Maritza and Trinity close ranks beside him, nodding but saying nothing.

"Enzo, let us handle this," Dad says, holding a hand up to stop Enzo from saying any more. But Officer Keith's face is red, and it's possible that Enzo just made things worse for me.

"Mr. and Mrs. Roth, I think it would be best if you brought your son down to the station tomorrow."

"I think it would be best if you saw your way to the door," Mom says to him, and Dad squeezes her hand, but he doesn't say anything.

Officer Keith smiles a humorless smile and tips an imaginary cap on his head.

"Thanks for your time," he says. "See you tomorrow."

Mom turns her back and faces the rest of us in the room. "Don't count on it," she mutters, and I'm tempted to think I'm out of the woods until she hears the front door close.

"What is the matter with you?" she hisses, and I instinctively back against the wall.

"I . . . I . . ."

I'm a highly sensitive adolescent prone to anxiety and heightened obsessive tendencies.

"Do you have any idea how much trouble you're in?" she asks, and Dad decides to answer for me.

"Oh, he knows."

I stare at the dozens of Missing posters, lying there at our feet, incriminating me in my own room. For a moment, I entertain the possibility that I really did do it. All that wandering in my sleep, maybe I was up to more than I realized. But why would I want to point the blame at myself? Unless I really am crazy.

Or someone wants me to look crazy.

"It's brilliant," I whisper, forgetting for a second that anyone else is there.

"Son, you're a lot of things, but 'brilliant' isn't what I'd be using to describe yourself in this moment," Dad says.

I look straight at him.

"It was him. It's been him all along!" I say.

"Narf—"

"Dad, he's done it before! The address book! He somehow got in here . . . I mean, I don't know how, but he must have snuck in—"

"Nicky, stop it," my mom says, looking angry or worried

or something else altogether. Afraid? I've never seen Mom afraid.

"Hold on, the address book from the kitchen?" Maritza says, catching on before anyone else.

"Exactly!"

I'm pacing now, shuffling the posters across the floor, and everyone picks their feet up so as not to step on the faces of the missing.

"He took the address book back. It was under my bed, and then he was standing out there with it, and . . . he must have somehow put these here, too!" I say, and whatever my face looks like, it can't be good, because suddenly, the room is full of wide, blinking eyes.

"Don't you see?" I yell, because how can they not see? "He's framing me!"

I look from my parents to my friends to my parents. It's official. They all think I did this. At least the tearing-down-the-flyers part. I can only hope they don't actually think I made Aaron and Mya disappear.

"I didn't do it!" I say, hoping that stands for everything.

It only just occurs to me that I have no idea why my friends are even here.

Mom's ready with an answer before I can ask, though.

"They came over to apologize," she says, clearly no longer thinking I deserve whatever apology they were ready to offer.

"So you called the police?" I ask, not meaning for it to come out like an accusation, but I can't manage to control a single emotion right now.

"We called the police because we were scared to death you'd gone missing, too!" Dad says, and this is the first moment I feel really, truly guilty. Not afraid I'll get into trouble. Not worried I won't be believed. Actual guilt for making them feel that feeling. Because if I miss my friends as much as I do, I can only begin to imagine how scared my parents were that they might have to get used to feeling that way about me.

"We were just looking for some hint of where you might have gone, and it was all under the bed, and . . ." Trinity says, and I think she's trying to be understanding because she is making an effort to look at me and not at the flyers, but her gaze always returns to the piles on the floor.

Maritza is who shocks me the most, though. Because her eyes are glossy with tears. She doesn't say a word to me. She just . . . hates me.

"I think you kids had better get home," Mom says, ushering the kids out. "I'll drive you."

She says it with a tone of protection I would give anything to feel right now. Now that she knows I'm safe, it's possible she may never talk to me again. It's possible I may not leave this room for the rest of my natural life.

And just to make sure I suffer a just punishment, she yanks the cardboard boxes filled with my dismantled gadgets and gears and sprockets and unpicked locks from my closet.

"You can kiss these goodbye, too. To the junk pile they go, along with anything else that's precious to you."

Dad leaves me with one lingering look, and this may be the look that drives the final stake through my almost-dead heart.

He's disappointed in me.

I don't even let myself sit on my bed. That would be too comfortable, and I'm positive I don't deserve that. Instead, I force myself to sit among the flyers of my lost friends, the only friends I might have left, and I'll never see them again. I know that now. Whatever happened to them, it started too long ago to stop, and if it hasn't ended already, it will end with or without me. It's completely, 100 percent out of my control. I mean absolutely nothing in this place.

I don't know if I cry myself to sleep or just wrestle with the knot in my throat until I pass out. All I know is that the last things I feel before I don't feel anything at all are the hard surface under me, the crinkling of paper against my skin, and the cold of a room that is lonelier than when I first moved to Raven Brooks.

Chapter 9

I'm not supposed to be outside. Everyone is asleep, and the air is alive with the sound of night. The way the wind flows through the trees sounds like a low whisper I might be able to hear if I could only stand still enough.

But I'm out here for the lightning bugs. They like to gather by the side of the yard where the weeds grow through the holes in the chain-link fence, where I catch Bubbe standing sometimes, staring into her coffee cup like she's looking for answers.

The lightning bugs dance and circle one another now, blinking their lights on and off like flashlights, and I hold my jar as high over my head as I can, hoping tonight will be the night I catch one to bring back into my room. My night-light never seems to glow bright enough.

But they go away too soon, lured by the whispers in the trees maybe, and I'm suddenly alone in the side yard, awake and disappointed.

I don't mean to start digging at first. It's just something

I do when I find a stick and soft ground. Once I've made a sizeable hole, I start thinking about things to bury, something that I could keep as a secret just for me, just like the trees have their secrets with the lightning bugs.

But the deeper my stick sinks, the harder it is for me to stop, and soon I'm scrambling to the edge of the yard because the hole I've dug has begun to overtake me. It's growing without my help.

Then the hole swallows me, and I'm falling . . . falling . . . until I land on a cold, hard surface surrounded by darkness.

When I look for the opening above me, I see only more darkness. The hole has swallowed me.

I grope my way through the slick walls of soft earth that feel too close to me. If I'm still enough, I almost think I can feel the walls inhaling and exhaling, moving toward me, then away from me.

While I'm standing still, I hear something beyond the breathing walls. I hear the soft sound of quiet sobbing.

I walk toward the glow of a white light that looks so much like the moonlight from the yard, I think I might have found my way out. Instead, I find the back of a boy, his legs tucked tight against him, his head resting on his knees.

"Hello?" I say, terrified that the boy will turn around, but somehow I know this is my only way out.

The boy turns to face me, and it's Aaron, his eyes wide with horror, his mouth taped over with a thick black X.

And still, even with the tape over his mouth, he manages to issue his desperate plea.

"Help me."

"I can't. I just can't anymore. I tried!" I tell him.

And this time, he does something new. This time, he reaches for the tape over his mouth and pulls one of the ends, tearing away the cover until I can see his lips move. But suddenly, it isn't Aaron's face anymore.

It's my grandma's.

She's sitting in her favorite recliner by the window, the sunlight shining through her thin silver hair, two fragile hairpins keeping the stray curls in place.

She's rocking slowly in her worn chair, her feet barely touching the ground as she points her toes to lift her back up, only to rock onto her toes again. I saw her a lot this way, but never in my dreams. Never at the surface of my memory.

She looks at me without blinking, but I'm not afraid. I'm not braced for the words she might hurl at me as some jumbled warning from her puckered mouth. I'm focused only on the steady creak of her chair as it rocks backward, forward, backward.

"Hi, Bubbe," I say, and it's so natural. I'd forgotten how natural it was to talk to her toward the end.

"Hi, Boychik," she says, her voice no longer gravelly. Right before she died, it was almost entirely gone, faded to a high whisper she could barely get out, but she always made the effort for me.

"Where have you wandered off to now, Little Wolf?" she asks me, even though I'm standing right there in front of her.

"I haven't," I tell her.

"Oh, but you have. You always do," she says. "Just remember, Boychik, you'll always be alone if you wander, unless . . ."

* * *

I wake not with a start, but with a groan.

The Missing posters have formed a sort of nest around me on the floor, but they provided no padding, and every bone in my body aches from marrow to skin.

My room is dark. Even the moon hides itself behind the clouds as the sky prepares for another storm.

I pull myself to my feet and walk slowly toward my window.

I don't know how long I stare across the street at the window I can see so clearly now. And I don't know when I decide that I have to go back to the factory. The only thing

I do know is that it's the worst possible idea, and I'm still doing it.

I feel my fingers slide underneath the screen and over the mesh. I feel the bite of blustery wind as it whips the tail of my shirt against my back. I feel the ledge of the window dig into my leg as I swing my body against the trellis. I feel the slat of the trellis that's been my ladder rung for nearly a full year now finally give out.

The wood snaps under my weight, and if it had a voice it would be telling me, "I warned you I'd break, but you didn't listen."

I land hard on my tailbone, the pain shooting up my spine to the base of my neck, but I manage to get to my feet without so much as a grunt because I'm that determined to get back to the factory.

The wind picks up even more, and a full-blown storm begins to brew. I make my way out of Friendly Court, and I have this feeling of dread that, whatever my street looks like now, I'm never going to see it the same way again. Something is different about this night.

At least half of me expects to find my equipment gone, the tapes re-smashed, my progress shattered. Mr. Peterson has made sure every one of my efforts fell apart, so why not this, too? Instead, the makeshift screening room is exactly as I left it, waiting for me to see the rest.

I crouch down to find the next tape. So far the things

I've seen, however horrific, have con-
firmed what I already knew: Mr.
Peterson had begun to unravel, and
his family was worried that he was
becoming unrecognizable. But then there was
the way Mr. Peterson shouted at Mya—I've never seen
him be angry at her like that.

I rehang the canvas on its nails and locate the last
dated tape.

"August twenty-second," I say, still anxious about why
the fourth tape hasn't been dated.

I put the August tape in and wait for the reel to catch, the
VCR struggling again to make sense of all the splicing.
Then the picture flickers to life on the tarp.

Except it's hard for me to tell at first that the picture has
actually come into focus. If not for the faint carnival music
in the background, I wouldn't have known that the reel had
actually begun. The picture is grainy and shaky, the space
nearly as dark as the security room I stand in now.
Accompanying the all-too-familiar carnival music, I hear
breathing. The person behind the camera is practically
hyperventilating.

The camera advances toward some sort of flickering
light at the end of what looks to be a hallway of some sort.
Maybe it looks familiar? I can't tell.

As the lens adjusts to the growing light, a picture pulls

into focus as the cameraperson rounds a corner. There, seated behind a massive desk cluttered with blueprints and news articles—materials I remember from a particular office in a particular house across the street—is the hulking back of Mr. Peterson. His office looks different, but he's as recognizable as ever.

He's hunched over his work, his hands pulling at the back of his neck and running roughly through his hair. Another sound joins the chorus of trembling breath and carnival music: the sound of Mr. Peterson mumbling an entire conversation to himself. Only parts of it are audible.

". . . can't go here or it'll . . ."

". . . no, no, no, no, that's impossible . . . but if we . . . yes, we could modify the . . ."

". . . don't understand me . . . never understood me . . ."

". . . it wasn't me. It wasn't me!"

Suddenly, Mr. Peterson's back goes rigid. The person behind the camera stops breathing altogether, and now it's just the carnival music.

Slowly, Mr. Peterson twists in his chair, and his entire face is revealed in all its maniacal terror. His mustache, normally curled in tight rings, is standing straight up at either side, like two bull horns jutting sky-ward. His eyes are saucers, bloodshot and twitching at the lower lid. His hand grips a pencil so hard that, when he turns, he snaps it in two without seeming to notice.

"Mya!" he growls, knocking over his chair as he charges toward the camera, and I instinctively back away from the canvas, just as Mya backed away while filming, turning to flee in the opposite direction.

I don't hear Mr. Peterson say anything else. I only hear the thunder of running feet, maybe Mya's or maybe her dad's, but the camera jostles and retreats back into the shadows where the video started. The flicker of light is gone now, and soon the sound is gone as well—the carnival music, the slapping of running feet. The only sound left is once again breathing.

Mya gasps and sputters, but the camera slows to a stop, then remains perfectly still. The last sound I hear before the camera cuts out completely is a tiny sob.

I was already dreading watching that last, undated tape. Something about its lack of marking made it feel that much more terrifying, as though to even name it would be to acknowledge it. After seeing this most recent footage, though, I wonder for the first time if I really do need to see it.

But this is what I've been searching for. For nearly a year, I've known that there were more mysteries across the street than the town of Raven Brooks was willing to admit. More was happening in that house—has continued to happen in that house—than the police, my friends, even *my own parents*, are capable of acknowledging.

And if these last three tapes don't already show that Mr. Peterson is still the most likely answer to the question of where Aaron and Mya are, then this tape will no doubt hold the most powerful evidence.

I eject the August tape and insert the unmarked VHS, bracing myself for what it shows me.

Yet nothing could have prepared me for what appears on the screen.

It's laughter. And light.

Mya is breathless. Her hands fumble with the camera at first. Her right forearm comes into the frame for a split second, but her laughter is unmistakable.

"Wait! Oh man, I think I hit the date button . . ."

She regains her grip on the camera, and the picture jostles as she launches into a run, her steps only slightly out of sync with the ones following her.

"I'm sorry, I'm sorry!" she calls, but it doesn't sound like she is. It sounds like she's proud of herself.

She stumbles at some point, the frame zooming in on the carpet I recognize from the Petersons' second floor. She stands again, and this time her voice isn't quite as victorious.

"Okay, I won't go in there again!" she says, and though some humor lingers in her tone, something else has crept in.

Her breathing grows stronger, and she shifts direction quickly, gulping for air before ascending a staircase down a hallway that I've never seen. She circles back to her own hallway, but the camera drops to her side for a minute, and the picture goes fuzzy. When it returns, she's in a dark room, panting and shuddering, her grip on the camera now pointing it toward a dark ceiling. I get the strong impression she's holding it against her chest, no longer concerned with recording. It makes it impossible to see where she is, but not how she feels.

I can hear her heart beating.

There's a clatter from somewhere off camera, and Mya is off again, this time looking out a window, and suddenly, she's outside. The camera pans its surroundings, and I see the inverted image of my family's turquoise house across the street. I see the top of the tree that stood outside of Aaron's room until yesterday.

"She's so high up," I breathe, trying to picture her balancing along the roofline of her house as she fled from someone that could make her laugh that freely, but suddenly make her fearful enough to get away.

I remember a moment in the Petersons' kitchen that moved quickly enough to give me whiplash. All that talk about bones and the way Mrs. Peterson got so quiet. I remember us waiting for Mr. Peterson to explode, only to watch him melt Mya into a puddle of giggles.

There's just one bone you can't live without . . . the funny bone!

If he could go from frightening to funny, couldn't he go from funny to frightening?

Mya's feet are crunching over the shingles as the image of my house grows closer.

She's backing away.

"Please, I don't want to play anymore," she says.

There is no more laughter in her voice. The picture wobbles as her feet move unsteadily across the roof. The sound of her Golden Apple charm bracelet clatters against the side of the camera as she trembles.

"I promise I won't. I promise—"

I can't tell if it's her who gasps or me or whoever was chasing her.

I can't tell how I fell to the floor of the security room.

I can't hide from what the lens shows me: grass.

It feels like I just fell three stories from the roof of the Peterson house, but that wasn't me. That was the camera.

That was Mya.

A light breeze blows the grass, bending the blades backward, capturing the camera's focus.

When the wind stops, the camera refocuses on Mya's

arm, her Golden Apple charm bracelet strapped to her wrist, her fingers curled, palm up, perfectly still.

I stare for what might be hours. It might be two minutes.

Thudding footsteps halt above the camera. My paralysis is shattered by a scream so primal, I cry with it. The agony travels from the canvas straight to my throat.

When the screaming stops, a voice so hoarse I can barely make it out asks her to wake up.

"Mya? Mya?"

But her fingers stay curled in their loose grip on the air. Mya is gone.

I think I shake my head. I think I bite my hand. I think I hold my knees to my chin and rock back and forth, but honestly, I don't know because I've gone completely numb.

The picture moves again. It moves away from Mya and away from the light. The picture returns to the dark.

It starts slow but then speeds up, and soon, the camera is running again, through the house via the kitchen door near the garbage cans, past the living room with its perpetually playing TV, down a set of stairs I remember finding by accident, down a hallway I should never have traveled, one with an office and a basement door now bolted with a red lock.

I see both doors, basement and office, but just as the lens starts to pull one of them into focus, the camera drops to the side of whoever is holding it, and a hand obscures the picture. There's some sort of movement, a rustling near the microphone, and at first, I think maybe we're traveling down a staircase. But when the hand finally pulls away, the camera is set on top of a familiar desk.

I immediately recognize Mr. Peterson's desk, the one cluttered with blueprints of impossible slopes and horrified faces.

I cringe as I wait for Mr. Peterson to appear before the camera to confess to what he's done. I wait for him to admit remorse. I don't want to see his face, but maybe if I could see him broken, maybe it wouldn't hurt so much to know that Mya is gone.

Instead, I hear a different voice, a voice so deep and full of loathing I almost don't recognize it. But it's Aaron's voice, and it drips with a hate I can almost feel physically.

"You're a monster," he accuses his father. I picture Mr. Peterson standing there before his son, surrounded by a madness of his own making, the evidence of his deteriorated sanity lying in scattered piles all around the camera.

"You're a monster."

Chapter 10

The security room in the factory has grown cold. I don't know if it's the storm that has begun to brew outside or the fact that it's the middle of the night.

Or the knowledge that Mya is gone, and Mr. Peterson is the reason why.

I have in my mind the absolute right thing to do. I've pictured it a million times since ejecting the last tape from the VCR. I should leave the factory immediately. I should go back to my house and ring the doorbell until my parents wake up. I'll risk their wrath again as I explain that I snuck out, that I broke the trellis, that I built a machine to view the reassembled tapes from the canvas bag (*What ingenuity I showed*, we could say when I'd be interviewed on the six o'clock news. *What determination!*).

Never mind that they were stolen tapes, recovered from the backyard of the neighbor I'd been explicitly told to stay away from. I should explain to them that I knew it was wrong, but Aaron and Mya were in danger, and wasn't that more important? And now we have proof that I was right, at least about Mya, and isn't that the most important of all?

I should tell them that all the evidence that's suddenly begun pointing toward me was meant to mislead them, to silence me, to keep the Peterson family secrets buried in the yard across the street. Mr. Peterson was behind it all: the flyers and the mannequin, all the misdirection last winter.

The right thing to do would be to tell them everything.

But I've spent the last year doing the right thing, and it's gotten me nowhere. The careful evidence I gathered with my friends was written off by the police. The alarm bells I raised with my parents landed me in weekly appointments with Dr. Fern. The snooping I did at the Peterson house got me framed for something I didn't do.

No more.

I'm going to save my friend, even if I have to do it myself.

I take the tarp down from the wall of the security room and neatly fold it. I set it beside the reanimated corpses of the VHS tapes, the VCR, the generator, and the now-empty canvas bag still covered in old dirt.

Then I leave the factory. I leave through the front doors, and I leave those doors wide open. Someone will find them open, and eventually, someone will find what I've already found. I welcome them in. I invite them to witness the family tragedy I've had to watch alone while everyone else insisted on moving on.

Coming Soon: Earth Pro Corporation's Street of Green!

I walk through the path in the woods that leads me to the old Golden Apple Amusement Park— now the EarthPro Corporation's Street of Green, a development that will run on clean energy but will never be rid of the dirty secret the park hid for so long.

Aaron knew it. Aaron saw it firsthand. And that's why Mr. Peterson made him disappear.

The wind whirls around me and rattles the leaves on their branches, and if the park's remains were still intact, I might be tempted to look over my shoulder in search of the beast that would follow me in my dreams, chasing me into the park to dig for secrets. But nothing of that park exists anymore, and there's nothing behind me but spliced-together tape and a distant roll of thunder.

What's ahead of me is what I'm more concerned with. Because what's ahead of me is Mr. Peterson, his house, and the answer once and for all about where Aaron is, and if Aaron even *is* anymore at all.

I'm not doing the right thing. I'm doing the only thing I can now. I have no choice, and I have no one in my corner. So I'll go alone.

My eyelashes catch the first scattered raindrops that make it past the tree line, and I blink them away. They drip down my face like tears, but these aren't tears. Tears would mean I'm sad for what I lost, but I'm not sad. I'm angry. I'm furious for what's been taken from me: friendship. What's left is just a vacuum, a fertile place for suspicion to grow. Maybe this is why Aaron always seemed to be kicking against an undercurrent of anger and exhaustion. Maybe he was also tired of losing what mattered to him . . . *who* mattered to him.

In fact, it occurs to me that the only person who could possibly understand this whole thing is Aaron. And Aaron might still be alive.

Heat rises above the collar of my shirt, and I'm suddenly impervious to the violent wind around me and the rain falling from above. I'm not hampered by the thunder and the lightning and the storm that seems to be telling me to turn back, to go home, to *move on.*

If it weren't so blatant, I might think it was just my imagination, but the minute I set foot onto Friendly Court from the path in the woods, the gusts of wind calm to near nonexistence. The entire street stills like it's centered in the eye of a hurricane, and I wait for something to happen. Because of course something will happen.

I watch a hard, rainbow-striped rubber ball roll from the side yard of the Peterson house—where the slats to the fence are missing—and into the street, coming to a standstill directly in front of my foot. It's the same ball from earlier, the one I nearly tripped over on my way back from the factory the first time. I bend to pick it up because that's what I'm supposed to do. It's like the entire play has been written for me.

As I hold the ball in my fist, right on cue, the wind picks back up, and once again, the storm is upon us. I turn to look at the turquoise house behind me, the one I saw from the camera lens before Mya fell. The house looks different now. It had begun to feel like mine. It really had. It was a feeling I never thought I'd have after calling so many houses "ours." But when it all fell apart, slowly, the turquoise house became just another place, just another rented address to lay down our heads until the next town.

I turn back to the Peterson house, and just as tightly as I hold the ball in my hand, I hold tight to the belief that Aaron is still alive, and he needs my help.

I wait for just the right rumble of thunder to erupt in the sky. Then I throw the ball through Aaron's closed window as hard as I can, the second time I've broken this very window.

A perfect, ball-sized hole forms in the lower corner of the window, jagged teeth of glass surrounding it. I run across the street and let myself into the side yard of the turquoise house and find what I'm looking for under the overhang—my boxes of parts Mom confiscated and added to the trash heap, just as she told me she would.

I empty every gear and sprocket and lock into the grass except for a few longer pieces strategically placed to help keep the boxes from caving under my weight, then drag them two at a time, swiping wet hair out of my face, and climb an old tool shelf Mr. Peterson left by the driveway. Then I stack the first box atop the second.

"You want to chop down a tree? Fine, I'll grow another one," I say through sputters and coughs because now the rain is blowing into my nose and mouth.

My makeshift ladder complete, I take a breath and move fast, knowing I won't have much time to test the integrity of my structure once I'm standing on it.

Rain pours down on me and on the boxes, and in no time, the cardboard begins to soak and soften, my weight beginning to collapse the stairs.

I look up, frantically searching for a foothold, and I find one in a downspout connected to the gutters that line the roof. Stretching my leg until it hurts, I can barely reach the downspout with the tip of my toe. If I'm going to make it, I'll have to jump. And if I jump, I have one shot at this.

I make my move before I'm ready. The box beneath me caves to the rain, and my foot finds the side of a radio I was using to prop the box up. With that as my springboard, I leap clumsily to the downspout. But the rain has made it slick and I have to alternate feet as soon as one slides off.

Determination and sheer, stupid luck keep me perched on a chunk of metal in the pouring rain.

I look for my next move and find it in the gutter. It's the

only thing I'm able to reach from my position, and at least it'll get me on a semi-flat surface.

Pull-ups were never really my thing. I could manage the one it takes to pass the PE exam in school, but that's about it.

"C'mon, Narf. It's just another day in PE," I say to myself, but I don't remember trying to do this in the rain while my feet play slip-and-slide on a slick piece of metal.

"Three, two . . . Aliens be with me," I say, and grasp the gutter, hoisting my body with a massive grunt muffled by a well-timed crash of thunder.

With the gutter now cutting into my gut, I flail my legs wildly, which somehow manages to propel the lower half of my body forward enough for me to push against the gutter and inch my way onto the roof.

The roof.

I stand and feel the full force of the storm. And I think about Mya.

But the storm is raging now, and I make a great lightning rod standing up here, so I crouch and look over the edge of the roofline to see if there's any way I can reach Aaron's window from here.

Moving toward the pitch of the roof, I start to slip and have to scamper back on my hands, my heart racing. I clamber for purchase and hang on for dear life, dropping my head over the side to make sure no one has noticed I'm up here.

I find myself face-to-face with the roof overhanging the doorway.

I'm going to have to jump again, but lucky for me, it looks like the angle of that side is less steep than it is over here. I crouch forward and hurl myself to the other ledge before I can think too hard about the height, and then leap again onto the small patch of roof just below Aaron's broken window.

"Now to get through it," I say, trying to picture it in my head before attempting it.

Suddenly, a blinding flash splits the sky, and an angry roar of thunder follows. I look down the street and watch as a tree's thick bark snaps like a toothpick, its top half tipping to the side and falling on top of a row of trash cans in the neighboring yard.

There's no more time for deliberation. I reach my hand through the jagged hole of Aaron's window and release the latch, pulling it up from the inside ledge while I try to ignore the way the jagged glass is slicing fine lines into my forearm.

With the window most of the way up, I wiggle the front part of my body forward and into the room before the slick roof begins to loosen its grip on me.

Another crack of thunder hides the sound of me falling the rest of the way through, and all at once, I'm on the floor in a big open room. This isn't Aaron's room anymore, though.

Mr. Peterson has transformed it: a row of shelves still

lines the wall on the right, but now a set of stairs that lead to nowhere split the room in two. To my left, a locked door sits beside a massive painting I don't recognize. When I nudge the painting, I see a hole in the wall leading to a small, dark room no bigger than a storage closet, the lattice on the window just over my head glowing with the outside light.

I look desperately for keys to the locked doors, my short-lived relief at escaping the roof succumbing to the claustrophobia of this space with two locked doors and stairs that lead to a wall.

Stairs to nowhere. Just like the Winchester Mystery House.

"Keys, keys . . . where are the keys?" I whisper.

If I'd been thinking clearly, I would have come prepared with my lockpicks.

If you'd been thinking clearly, you wouldn't be here at all.

I shoo away the unhelpful voice and scan the room for anything resembling a key. A sliver of light falls on the wall beside the hole leading to the small room, and there on a hook dangles a key clearly not meant for a door. It looks more like a car key.

I stuff it into my pocket and frantically search the room, feeling my way along the unlit walls and floor until my fingers drag across something cold—a key perfect for a lock in the door connecting Aaron's room to the small one.

With that room open, I search the small side room, but if there's a key in here, it's lost to the shadows.

What were you hoping to find, a flashing neon arrow spelling out "THIS WAY TO AARON"?

But it wouldn't have been much weirder than this scenario. It's like I'm playing some sort of twisted carnival game, and the only way to get to the end is to . . .

. . . follow the trail.

It's a different voice in my head now, teetering on the edge of familiar. But I can't quite place it.

Lightning cracks outside, and a sudden flash of light illuminates the lever on the wall.

"What?"

I peer into the room that was once Aaron's and see that a similar lever has been installed higher on the wall in there, too.

"So no key, but . . ."

I have nothing to lose. I pull the lever by my foot and race through the hole in the wall to pull the other lever right after.

I briefly imagine one of the walls inverting and opening to reveal one of those hidden rooms rich villains always seem to have in spy movies. Instead, when I pull the lever, I hear from somewhere inside the walls a set of gears begin to grind. I put my ear to the wall to be sure, but I've heard enough gears in my tinkering to know. Then I feel the wall begin to vibrate.

Something is moving.

I press my ear to the wall and follow the sound of movement, but it sounds like it's farther, on the other side of the house. I back through the hole in the wall and out onto the roof, scrambling back the way I came. Sure enough, the left side of the house reveals a platform that has risen up beside Mya's room.

"Of course," I say, rubbing my head because honestly, how much weirdness can one house hold? Steeling my courage, I leap for the platform, barely managing to make it.

My answer awaits me in Mya's perfectly preserved room. It's nothing short of a shrine to the girl who used to want to be like her mom, dancing with a lightness her family couldn't give her.

The flowered wallpaper and purple rug were exactly as she left it, her bunk bed—a perfect match to Aaron's— standing to the right of the room, her old crayon drawings from second grade still hang on the walls. I spot her old guitar on the floor, a pang of sadness quickly snuffed out by the stomach-turning reality of what happened to her.

I want to leave the room, but something on the table by the window catches my eye, something that was important enough to scrawl on a scrap of paper and leave for me in a place only I would find it.

There on the table by the window is a red key.

I push the lump from my throat at the sight of it. I know

now that it couldn't have been Mya who left me the note, but seeing the key here makes it all the more real. Whoever left me that note was sending out their final cry for help— one more SOS. Aaron already knew what his father had done. He needed someone to know. He needed *me* to know.

I walk to the key slowly, like I'm expecting the floor underneath me to give way to a trapdoor. It wouldn't be the weirdest thing to happen in this house.

But the floor does not swallow me, and I grasp the key, holding it like a long-lost artifact, before tucking it away in my pocket, knowing that my next task will be the hardest.

I have to make my way downstairs without getting caught. I have to get to the basement door.

Mya's bedroom door is wedged shut with a chair, which I now move aside.

"This is what you came here to do," I tell myself.

I leave Mya's room, the key pressing against the side of my leg as my wet clothes cling to my skin. The door leads back into the small closet space and then into Aaron's room. From this angle, I can see a switch by my foot over the staircase. More gears grind and the wall at the foot of the stairs moves aside.

The house is colder than I've ever felt it before, and I'm telling myself that's why I have to stick my tongue between my teeth to keep them from chattering. I'm just cold.

Somehow, this is the first time I'm fully aware that I have zero strategy. I've managed to get inside. Anger and injustice propelled me that far.

I step lightly, the carpet not enough to suppress the squeak of floorboards I disturb. With each creak underfoot, I bite the tongue that's supposed to be muffling my chattering. I steel myself against the new dread that lies below on the ground floor: a thud that beats like a heartbeat from somewhere in the house.

I take the stairs one slow step at a time, my rain-soaked sleeve dripping tiny puddles onto the floor.

I can hear the static from the television in the sitting room, its programming failing under the power of the storm that rages outside. Wind leans on all sides of the house, but the walls are impervious to the violence outside. Whatever this place is made of, it's able to keep most of the sound out.

Which means it can probably keep most of the sound in.

The thudding is getting louder, and now that I'm closer to its source, I hear that it's not so much a repetitive thud as it is a rotating crash, like when my dad puts his running shoes in the dryer.

Lightning flickers outside, lighting up the house and then plunging it into darkness. I'm halfway across the downstairs hallway at the back of the house when another bolt lights the sky, and in the sudden light, I see something from the corner of my eye.

Someone is staring at me.

I leap back hard enough to catch my shoulder on the opposite wall. But I quickly realize no one is beside me. I'm standing next to a painting of a massive eyeball.

"Which means the basement door is . . ."

I don't even need the light from the storm to see it. The dull shine of the red padlock permeates the dark.

I jam my hand into my pocket and retrieve the red key from Mya's room.

In the space of a breath, I've fitted the key and turned the lock, wincing as the padlock falls to the floor and releases the basement door.

The basement.

"So here we are," I say to the forbidden doorway. Since the first time I set foot in this house, I knew this door and what lies beyond were off-limits. Now there's no going back.

"You'd better be down there, Aaron."

I poke my toe into the void, searching for the first step, and when I find it, it's a lot lower than I expect it to be. I wobble for a second, bracing myself against the railing on either side. If I don't hold on to something, my legs might give out.

There's a light on above me, but whatever waits at the bottom of the steps is steeped in darkness.

The thudding is louder than ever, and its unsteady rhythm is unnerving me. I'm not dripping from the rain outside anymore, but I swear I still feel something fall around me in puddles. It must be the last of my adrenaline.

I take another step into the darkness, and for the first time, I seriously think of turning back. No one knows I'm here. If I slip out now, I could make it back to my room no worse off than I started.

Except "where I started" was where we left it tonight—with everyone thinking I'm crazy or evil or crazy evil.

No, the only way forward is down.

The next step is the last one I see. Suddenly, the door at the top of the basement stairs slams shut, and I'm swallowed in complete darkness.

"No no no!"

I run back up the two steep steps and turn the handle, but the door won't budge. I thrust my shoulder against it, but something's barred it shut.

Or *locked* it shut.

"Hey! Let me out! Hey!"

I consider all the ways the door could have shut on its own. The place is old and drafty. One open window could have created the perfect vacuum to close the door.

To lock the door, too?

My legs shaking, I descend the stairs, closer and closer to the angry thuds below.

It feels like they go forever, but when I finally get to the last step, I don't feel relief. I'm on level ground, but it's barely any brighter at the bottom.

There's a boiler to my right in the tiny room, and a washing machine on my left.

I reach toward the washing machine and open the door, examining the washing machine for some sort of clue. But the answer is staring me right in the face.

"What is that?" I breathe, leaning into the machine to get a better look at the room in the back of the washer.

The basin is deeper than I expect—more like one of those you'd find in a laundromat—and I have to lean way in to see what it is I'm looking at.

Then I feel a push.

One strong hand, one strong shove, and the washing machine door closes behind me.

"Hey!" I yell. "HEY!"

I lean against the side of the machine and kick the door with my legs, but it doesn't budge. Instead, I tumble backward like a wet heap of laundry onto another cold surface.

I lie motionless on the floor looking up at a door before me. My shoulder hurts where I landed on it, and my shin is burning with what I suspect is a sizeable gash.

But pain is meaningless as soon as the reality of what's happened kicks in.

Someone pushed me into that machine. A wild panic seizes me, something primal that unravels any semblance of cool I might have had up to this point.

"Help! HELP!" I scream, and at first, the sound of my voice horrifies me, but once I've let loose the cry for someone to find me, I can't stop.

"Someone help me! HEY! Someone! ANYONE!"

I have heard of fight or flight, but pure, paralyzing terror should be an option as well. It's the kind of fear that makes you want to ricochet off walls, clawing your way toward a light switch or a window or an opening of some kind, anything that could lead you to a place other than where you are in that moment, but you can't. You're just stuck.

I lean back into the machine and push the door of the washer, but it's locked in place. I run myself in circles like a lab rat until I'm hoarse and exhausted, and only then do I grab hold of the little beast of irrationality inside of me and try to reason with it. I want to know what on earth I was thinking when I snuck into this house, and how on earth I'm going to get out of it.

My only choice is the gleaming door before me, opposite the opening in the wall where the washing machine let me in.

I choke back the panic rising up in my throat and grope for the door handle.

The room on the other side of the door is illuminated by

a few candles, dripping wax and dim light on the floor.

Which means someone's been here recently.

I spot a thin mattress on the floor of an otherwise bare room.

Which means someone's been sleeping here.

And though there are two "windows" against the wall closest to the mattress, their sunny scene doesn't seem to be bringing in enough light.

I grab the candle from the ground and hold the wavering flame closer to the scene outside, only to find that it isn't outside at all. Behind the pane of glass is a panel, painted to look like a sunny day on Friendly Court.

I put my face up against the glass and find the seam of the "window," but it reveals nothing on the other side except more darkness.

Like a staircase to nowhere.

Suddenly, I can't find a way out of this room fast enough.

I consider my options. I try to decipher what's on the other side of the mystery window, but it's anyone's guess in this nightmare mystery maze.

After looking for a latch and finding none, I turn to the only thing in the room I can use to break the glass: a basketball. I pluck the ball from the ground, take several steps back, aim, and throw.

My first two throws fail to break the glass, but the third shatters the window completely.

Candle in hand, I climb through the window and hold the light up to the next room, my feet crunching over broken glass.

It's not so much a room as it is a sort of antechamber behind the walls. Exposed pipes run along the walls and ceiling like veins, and if the mold stunk in the last space, this place is giving stench a whole new meaning.

I try to breathe through my mouth as I search for the next doorway. What I find instead is most unnerving of all: A dungeon gate just like the one in Scream School blocks the doorway across the room.

"This is a . . . cage," I hear myself say, but I can't figure out if it's a cage to hold something in or keep something out.

As I creep toward the gate, I try to see what stands on the other side, but I'm once again met with darkness. I try holding the candle up to the bars, but all I manage to do is create shadows unsettling enough to make me abandon that tactic altogether.

Across from the door I see a power switch. I try flipping it, but it only plunges the room further into darkness. But there's another switch to the right of the doorway. I have no choice. It's this dark corridor that may lead to freedom or the one behind me that definitely will not.

I pull the lever, and with far too much noise for my comfort, the gate slowly rises. I flatten myself against the wall underneath the lever in preparation for whatever beast I might have just freed, but when the gate finishes its journey upward, the air around me is once again still, and I reach for the candle at my feet.

That's when the few remaining raindrops clinging to the hem of my shorts land directly on the flame of the candle, extinguishing the only light that would have kept me from plunging into yet more darkness.

"Brilliant."

I stumble through the doorway beyond the gate and twist and turn through the next maze of corridors, following the wall with each bend and turn. Terror has utterly exhausted me. Between the whole clinging-to-the-roof-for-my-life thing and screaming-for-help part, I am just about ready to unravel. I'm once again moving downward, the floor sloping lower with each turn in the maze, but I can barely register it anymore. My legs are Jell-O, and I want nothing more than to rethink this entire plan from the warmth and comfort of my bed, even if it means never leaving my room again.

Just when I think I can't take another step, I do, and this time, I kick something hard enough to send pain shooting through my toe.

I listen to whatever I kicked roll to a stop on the floor, then drop to my hands and knees in pursuit of it because I've heard that sound before. I *know* that sound. It's the sound of a flashlight rolling like a Weeble on the ground.

My knee knocks into it again, and I grasp the handle quickly, feeling for the switch and welcoming the yellow glow of light in the darkness.

The beam lands squarely under the chin of a pale face with wide, unblinking eyes.

I scream before I can muffle it, and it takes me another minute to regain feeling in my hands because apparently that's what oxygen deprivation does.

If this mannequin was supposed to be guarding something, I couldn't say what because all I find beyond it is corridor after corridor in an endlessly winding series of doors, each leading me farther and farther down as the sound of the storm outside fades, giving way instead to the sounds of machinery and the hum of a massive generator rattling the floor beneath me.

"I could turn back," I tell myself.

And I could. Except that I'm not sure I could even find my way back at this point.

I press a switch on the generator, turning the light on top of it to green. But there's something else in this room—a fenced-in area at its center. I climb the fence to the other side, and find another dungeon gate blocking the door. I flip the switch and the gate rises. Beyond the door, I do find something different. Instead of the wallpaper and pipes, I feel the fine grooves of plywood and corkboard, two-by-fours and rusted nails, jutting from exposed beams.

I shine the flashlight against the walls and find that the whole hallway is covered in boards. Black muck-like tar fills the spaces between the slapped-together boards, and grease like lubricating oil is smudged in fingerprints all over the plywood.

What I notice the most, though, is the way the boards are slapped together and overlapped, like they might lead to freedom, like they needed to be tarred shut to prevent me from getting—

"Outside," I whisper, afraid to scare away the possibility that I might be close to escape. I drag my tired legs down the hallway and begin shining the flashlight all over, looking for a way out.

Suddenly, I hear the door behind me open, and my flashlight falls upon an impossibly tall figure. I feel the blood drain from every part of my body.

Mr. Peterson looms at the end of the corridor, obscured in shadow except for the mad glow of his wide, frantic eyes. I back away too fast, stumbling over a crack in the floor, and fumble with the flashlight just in time to duck away from the swooping arm that reaches for me.

I can hardly see where I'm going, and the flashlight beam is bouncing wildly across the walls I travel. There's no way out. I feel like a rat in a lab experiment.

I hear someone yelling—screaming—and at first, I think it's him, but the fire in my throat tells me it's me.

Just then, the beam of the light catches the corner of a doorway at the end of the corridor. Three locks seal it shut tight, but I'm not about to let them stand in my way.

I bring the metal flashlight down hard, hard, *hard* on each one. The power of the hit rattles through my hand as each lock falls to the floor, busted open.

"Come on come on come on!"

But in the end, it's the door itself that won't budge. I throw my entire weight against the door, but it's no use. The door refuses to open. I risk a look over my shoulder and see the top of an approaching shadow. He's close.

I look down at the knob and search for a keyhole, for any reason why I can't open the door, but all I see is the smooth surface of the doorknob.

Maybe the lock is on the other side of the knob.

Maybe the door is warped shut.

Maybe something's blocking it from behind.

I grip the knob tight and twist until my palms burn, but all I manage to do is loosen the actual knob from the door.

"That'll do."

I flip the flashlight around and hold the handle high overhead, bringing the butt down on the metal knob as hard as I can.

Unfortunately, I also bring the handle down on the thumb I wasn't quick enough to move.

Dizzy from the pain, I double over and bite my lip as

hard as I can to keep from screaming. In the silence, I hear the slow approach of Mr. Peterson's boots as he searches the dark corridor for me. He'll know I've turned here. He knows these halls in ways I never could, but he can't know exactly where the alcove is if he's in the dark like I am.

I set aside my pain and quickly flip the switch of the flashlight.

Steady now, Narf.

My hands shake and my palms sweat. Once again, I bring the butt of the flashlight high over my head, praying to every Alien in space that I connect with the handle and not another vital body part.

The sound of footsteps is so close, I can feel the ramp under me dip with Mr. Peterson's weight.

Clink!

The knob falls to the floor with a thud, and for a second, all is still under the echo of metal hitting wood.

Then I hear an unearthly growl and the pounding of footsteps on the ramp behind me.

I fling the door wide and kick the knob inside the room in front of me, then throw the door closed and switch the flashlight on. A large board rests on a hinge inside the room, and I push it to land in its resting place across the door just in time for two giant thuds to rattle the door in its frame. Then, in a standoff with the door and its bar between us, I hear Mr. Peterson's boots retreat.

When I turn around, I see lit by two more dripping candles a familiar scene, one I saw through the grainy footage of spliced-together VHS tape.

Mr. Peterson's desk is indeed larger than life, just as I remember it when I got lost in this house one year ago. Only at that time, the office was on the first floor.

You've changed. Ever since you moved your workshop down there, you've changed.

The desk looks oversized, even for a man of Mr. Peterson's stature. The back of the chair looms high, but it's no match for the massive desk it's paired with. If it's possible, the surface of the desk is even more cluttered than it was in the home movie, first with Mr. Peterson seated at it, then with Aaron beside him.

I move slowly toward the desk, Aaron's tormented accusation ringing in my ears.

You're a monster.

Littering the surface of the desk are the same articles with pictures of a young Aaron lingering in the background of the Golden Apple Amusement Park construction. Just like before, his image is circled in angry red ink, only this time, instead of cryptic labels like "OMEN," there's new writing on the photocopied pages, notes scrawled beside the pictures containing the theories of a madman:

Present at groundbreaking
Correlation to opening day??

First to ride Rotten Core. He already knew?

And then there's a note that doesn't point to any picture or article or angry red circle. In all capital letters, on a faded, curled Post-it:

The roof. Correlation to heights???

The roof.

I look at all the circled pictures and the writing beside them. Is that the same handwriting I remember seeing scrawled on these papers months ago? It looks so different.

I shuffle through page after page on the desk.

Day 30 of building: on-site accident–Present

Day 109 of inspection: electrical fire–Present

Cleaning crew accident on amphitheater awning: Really an accident??

And then, as I clear the last page from the pile and tear my brain apart trying to decipher the cryptic code of the scribblings I thought I recognized, I see something I could never have expected.

My own reflection.

I'm soaked and wide-eyed and pale, and the sight of my own face is startling enough. But what's more startling is the existence of a mirror on the surface of this desk at all. The glass is etched with a personalized message across the top:

Never lose your shine. Love, D

A gift from Mr. Peterson's wife, Diane. The mirror is

nothing more than a paperweight, its reflective surface meant as a reminder of how much his wife once loved him and his creative genius.

At some point, though, it must have become a reminder of what that genius had turned him into: a monster.

Except . . .

"Except it was Aaron standing here when he said that," I say, hypnotized by the memory of that very last VHS tape.

You're a monster, he'd said as he stood in this very spot. I'd assumed that Mr. Peterson was the one sitting here in this chair, but he didn't actually appear on camera at all.

I think of the way Mya laughed as she began with the upper hand, the camera tucked by her side as she ran away, victorious.

She'd snuck up on Aaron while he was drawing, while he was trying to escape the torment of his father's descent into insanity.

This is what I do to escape.

"Because he thought he was a curse," I mumble, leafing through the rambling notes scribbled across the image of a little boy watching his father's genius melt into something else.

"You were calling yourself a monster."

Which means . . . it was *Aaron* that Mya was running away from on the roof.

It was Aaron.

I back away from the desk.

I back myself all the way against a wall and slide to the floor as my brain rushes to make sense of what I've found.

Images and memories bombard me in an avalanche, burying me in thoughts of muted mannequins and sketches of anguished guilty faces scrawled on the backs of posters torn down by the very person responsible for his sister going missing. I think about the tapes crushed and hidden in the backyard, the warning to stay away from him that day after his mother died, the smear of blood on the note that floated from his window.

I squeeze the sides of my head to stop the memories from stacking up in my brain, but it's no use. All this time, it's been Aaron. How could I have been so wrong? What if his dad was just an innocent player in the world's most horrific game? What if there is no monster?

But that doesn't explain everything—why Mr. Peterson went digging in the park, why he lied to the police and everyone else . . .

It isn't adding up.

I grab the flashlight and drag myself to the back of the room with the desk and chair and scan the walls for another way out. A narrow door looms in the corner, locked from the inside, and I twist the lock and hold my breath, but all that lurks on the other side are more shadows. The next part of the maze.

This time, I enter a room filled with candles. Only a few actually hold a flame on their wicks, but it's enough for me to see two distinct memorials in separate corners of the room: one dedicated to Diane Peterson, and one to Mya. Mrs. Peterson's picture is barely visible behind a stack of decaying flowers and a thin gold necklace with a small, cracked heart charm on the end of it. The other half of the charm lies next to the half that dangles from the crumbling stem of one dead flower.

Mya's tribute is lined with stuffed animals worn with love and stained with age. From the ear of one particularly loved elephant hangs the tarnished gold bracelet with a tiny Golden Apple charm hanging from the clasp. And beside the elephant: a smaller version of the photograph of Lucy Yi. This one with hearts drawn around Mrs. Peterson and Mya, running to meet up with Lucy and Maritza.

There is a part of me that doesn't want to leave this room. I can see how whichever of them built these memorials— Aaron or Mr. Peterson—intended them to be a place to remember, a place to think about the times that didn't involve paranoid fights or cruel nicknames or the slow deterioration of a family.

I would stay here. But that would mean never leaving this part behind. It would mean lingering in the sadness that grief needs to thrive. I can't linger anymore. A body and a mind and a heart can only take so much.

I may not like what I find, but this search has to end. One way or another, I'll find the secrets Aaron and his father have buried in this house.

I pass through two more doorways and descend a ramp before I hear the tinny sound of carnival music traveling through a faraway speaker.

And soon, the music isn't that far away at all.

"Come one, come all, to the Land of Under! You'll flip your lid, you'll tip your hat, you'll spin your top!"

Mr. Peterson's voice booms over the music, a carnival barker of the original class, his laugh maniacal and unrestrained.

I am on a landing above a nightmare world.

Dozens of pale mannequins on tiny spinning wheels whir across the grounds below, zigzagging past one another in wobbly pursuit of work. One stocks the shelves of a concession stand garishly painted in primary colors. One pushes a shopping cart full of gears and flashing lights, parking it beside another one that yanks the wires from a ride and sets sparks flying as it repairs a control panel.

Another rotates a Ferris wheel that must be three stories high, its empty cars swinging wildly as the wheel speeds round and round.

"You're just in time for the games, Nicky boy!"

Mr. Peterson cackles into the speaker, the feedback creating earsplitting pops of static.

I back myself against the wall of the landing as I try to understand the chaos I'm witnessing, but it's simply too much to take in. I see what I think are roller coaster cars robbed from the old Golden Apple Amusement Park and the half-charred remains of stuffed animals that must have come from the prize stand. A group of faceless, wheeled mannequins busily sort spare parts on a table in a far corner while the carousel I watched come to life that night in the forest with Mya now spins at a speed far too fast in the distance.

And there is distance. And height. And depth. There's seemingly no end to this underground amusement park built for who knows what.

Or who knows *who*.

I scan the outer walls for a place to escape, but everywhere I turn is blocked by chain-link fence and barbed wire, iron gates like the dungeon-style door from above, or emotionless white mannequins tasked with standing guard in the gaps.

It's a prison fairground.

"This can't be real. This is a dream. Wake up, Nicky. Wake up!"

"It's your wildest dream come true, Nicky, my boy!" Mr. Peterson's voice booms. "Now step right up and join in the games. You're going to have fun Fun FUN!"

I'm going to run Run RUN!

I fly down the stairs and knock over two wheely mannequins that obstruct my path before reaching one of the fences. I hop onto the chain links and begin to climb to what might be freedom, but I can't say for sure because whatever's on the other side is shrouded in darkness.

"Uh-uh-uh," Mr. Peterson admonishes, and I can hear his finger wagging at me from wherever he's watching. "The razor wire's a doozy!"

He laughs so hard, the speaker crackles and fizzles out momentarily, leaving behind only the carnival music that can't seem to find its proper speed, as though it's playing on a record player that can slow to a warble or speed to a chipmunk tenor.

I climb down and back away from the fence, pressing myself against the concession stand just as the voice of Mr. Peterson returns to the speaker.

"Welcome home, Nicky. Welcome home."

But that's insane. This isn't home. This was never home.

I duck under the awning of the concession stand and shake my head until I'm dizzy.

This isn't happening. This can't be happening.

I can feel my head getting light, and I stop long enough to pull in one deep breath, then another, and for just a second, the sound of the tinny music and the whir of machinery recedes to the background, and I think that maybe I won't pass out, which right now would be a win.

Then, as I pull in my third breath, I hear an exhale from somewhere in the shadows of the concession stand.

I try to move. I try to drag myself away from the sound of the breathing, but it's no use. Fear has taken me over body and soul, and I have no control. I'm nothing more than a lump of flabby muscle.

"He wanted me to have a friend."

Feeling returns to my body like an electrical current. That voice. I know that voice.

A smallish, thin shadow with a tangle of short, wild hair rises on the wall beside me before pouring onto the basement floor.

"Aaron?"

"He wanted me to have a friend, but I don't deserve one. I don't deserve anything. I killed her, Nicky. I killed my own sister."

A buzzing starts in my ears, and that fainting feeling returns.

Then I remember.

I remember why I climbed up the wall and onto the roof and through the window and into the house. I remember why I turned away from everything safe and risked it all to find the only other person who I thought might understand me.

Even if he—

"It was an accident," I say. I don't even give him the option of arguing. "You would never do that to her, Aaron. You loved her."

Aaron is quiet for so long, I think maybe I imagined him there in my delirium.

Then, in a voice so quiet I can barely hear him over the music, Aaron says, "He just wanted to protect me. In his own horrible way, he wanted to protect me. I'm the only one he has left. That's why he won't let me leave."

"It was an accident, Aaron."

"I thought it was," he says. "I know I didn't mean to do it. But he's right, Nicky."

"Right about what?" I ask, barely getting the words out.

"Don't you remember what I told you? *I make bad things happen.*"

"Welcome to my greatest creation, lads! My greatest creation ever!" Mr. Peterson says through the speaker.

My brain scrambles for answers. There has to be something more. There has to be a clue I've missed, a lock I haven't picked, an answer I haven't dug up yet. This can't be it.

"Soon the world will know, and the critics will howl with delight at the return of Theodore Masters Peterson!"

The critics will howl.

Howl.

You'll always be alone if you wander, Little Wolf. Unless . . .

. . . unless . . .

. . . unless . . . you leave a trail.

They are Bubbe's words, the ones I finally remember now that nightmares have become reality.

But what trail have I left? I bulldozed over every trail I could have scattered behind me. There are the tapes in the factory, but that's going to get demolished any day now. There are the boxes outside of the house that I stacked to climb inside, but they've probably blown away with the storm.

There's Enzo and Maritza and Trinity and my parents and Officer Keith, but not a single one of them believes that there's anything to actually find in the Peterson house. Not really.

And besides, who could ever imagine the depths of insanity Mr. Peterson had to plumb to invent this nightmare? Who could imagine Aaron would be responsible for Mya's death, accident or not?

Who would believe I'd be stupid enough to follow every breadcrumb Mr. Peterson left for me to get me to this moment, just so Aaron could have a friend in this home-made prison?

"I didn't leave a trail. I . . . wandered."

Mr. Peterson left just enough evidence to incriminate me and divert all the attention to a troubled loner who's moved around so much, he's lost all sense of what's normal. A teenager who got so mad at his parents and his friends that he up and left one night, breaking the trellis on his way out of town, a canvas duffel bag missing from his room that he no doubt packed to run away from home.

Aaron is right next to me, but he sounds so far away.

"I warned you, Nicky," he says. "I told you not to come back."

And in this glaring moment of clarity, I realize that I've unearthed the long-hidden secrets of the Peterson family. I've unburied their skeletons, and in their place, I've buried myself.

And no one is ever going to find me.

About the Author

Photo credit: Kristyn Stroble

CARLY ANNE WEST is the author of the YA novels *The Murmurings* and *The Bargaining*. She holds an MFA in English and Writing from Mills College and lives with her husband and two kids near Portland, Oregon. Visit her at www.carlyannewest.com.

ISBN 978-1-338-34859-0

10 9 8 7 6 5 4 3 2 1   19 20 21 22 23
Printed in the U.S.A.   23

First printing 2019
Book design by Cheung Tai